I0557090

Nyx: The Protectors
by Tyree Campbell

Copyright © 2012 by Sam's Dot Publishing

Cover art "Nyx on the Shore" Copyright © 2012 by Laura Givens

Cover design by Laura Givens

All rights reserved. No part of this book may be reproduced or transmitted in any form or by any means, electronic, mechanical, including photocopying, recording, or by any information storage and retrieval system, without the written consent of the publisher, except by a reviewer who wishes to quote brief passages in connection with a review written for inclusion in a magazine, newspaper, broadcast, etc.

Nyx: The Protectors is works of fiction. Names, characters, places, and incidents are products of the author's imagination. Any resemblance to actual events or persons, living or dead, is entirely coincidental.

SAM'S DOT PUBLISHING
P. O. Box 782
Cedar Rapids, Iowa, 52406-0782

www.samsdotpublishing.com

First printing March 2012

By Tyree Campbell

Novels
The Dog at the Foot of the Bed
The Dice of God
The Quinx Effect
The Breathless Stars [in 2012]

Novels in the Nyx Series
Nyx: Malache
Nyx: Mystere
Nyx: The Protectors
Nyx #4 [in 2012]

Novellas
The Martian Women

Novelettes
Cloudburst
Sarrow [in 2012]

Collections
A Nice Girl Like You [published by
Bedazzled Ink]

Graphic Novels
Pyra and the Tektites, Vol. 1
[with Teri Santitoro]
Pyra and the Tektites, Vol. 2
[with Teri Santitoro] [in 2012]

For the Noble Pen writers' group . . .

. . . of Scott's Family Restaurant, Cedar Rapids, Iowa, the invaluable critiques and insights of whose members helped keep the narrative on target.

001

You'd think that someone in my profession, given a ten-day furlough, would seek out a nice, quiet spot on some remote and sparsely-populated world and attempt to, as they say in the travel'grams, get away from it all, from all the death and violence associated with duties as an operative for an interstellar agency that does not officially exist. Would watch a sunset on a beach, have a drink, perhaps find someone compatible for the rest of the night, if not for the sojourn. Indeed, my idea of an evening involves several fingers of a single malt and two or three cherry cheroots, and I'd already indulged rather well by the time the pale red sun had sunk halfway toward the horizon of Adenne, as the world I had selected for my furlough is known. A few beachcombers were about, picking at shells and detritus, none paying any mind to me sitting in the beach chair well back from shore. Not that I'd planned on attracting attention--I was wearing, if it matters, a sleeveless green top loose and long enough to conceal the Krupp-Stern 506 tucked under the waistband of a pair of cammie trousers cut off at mid-thigh--but I hadn't reckoned that I would be ignored. Even slouching I sat tall in the chair-- at 192 centimeters, it's difficult not to--and perhaps no one was in the offing for a long, skinny woman like me. Perhaps the strings of algae washed ashore by the tide were more alluring or interesting.

I was about to light another cheroot and revel in solitude when something kicked up a patch of sand about three meters off my right foot.

In our line of work a certain amount of assault is expected. One might go so far as to say that assault *is* our line of work, except we max out our efforts. More to the point, we Blacklight operatives are not invulnerable, and if we can hunt down and dispatch targeted individuals, the same can be done to us. That seems only fair. Deven, however, does not expect us to be fair, merely efficient. In this instance, ducking for cover seemed the better part of efficiency.

One of the drawbacks to beaches is that they are generally lacking in cover for which to duck. I knew what had impacted in the sand, of course, and already had hunched my shoulders involuntarily in anticipation of another bullet from the high-powered rifle as I dove off the chair and to my left. I had heard no report, which suggested the weapon was equipped with a sound suppressor. Some two hundred meters inland ran a line of broken bluffs, geologically an ancient, eroded escarpment, that doubtless concealed my assailant. His hold on the high ground made a circuitous approach problematic, as it would provide him with opportunities to lead me properly and pick me off. I didn't bother drawing my Stern; the range-to-dissipation of its blue beam was one-eighth the distance it would have to travel. I had but two options, both of which required me to run for a couple hundred meters: either bring myself within range, or take myself well out of his.

After a couple rolls over the sand I sprang to my feet and began a dash toward the low ridgeline in an irregular weaving pattern that, I hoped, would make it nearly impossible for him to adjust his sights quickly enough to compensate. A faint flash of movement on the crest suggested that he had fired again. I flinched, but in the second it took to do so the bullet had already passed me by without effect. I cut right, then dodged left, and reached the end of the sand and the beginning of a field of tufts of dry grass strewn with bits of gravel that stabbed at my bare soles. Off to the right I spotted a hikers' trail that looked as if it led to the top of the bluffs, some twenty meters above beach level. It would afford me some cover if I could reach it. At fifty meters from the trail I spotted another movement, and the indistinct shape said that the downward angle had now reached the point where he was compelled to stand and reveal his position in order to fire. After another five running steps I took out the Stern and sent a blue burst in his direction just as he rose to shoot again, and he pulled back, though the beam diffused at least ten meters in front of him. Five more steps brought me to the cover of the escarpment.

The ascending trail wound back and forth to accommodate random protrusions of granite. The climb was slow, because I had to tread carefully on the rough surface while keeping an eye on the crest above. At perhaps five meters from the top, a thin, high-pitched whine reached my ears, and I paused behind a massive boulder, peering carefully around it. The whine increased in intensity, and then gradually faded. I surged upward, Stern ready, and reached the top of the bluff just in time to see the airfoil disappear down the glideway that led through the woods and toward the small resort town of Sayoun some four kilometers away.

Thoroughness demanded that I inspect the firing site cautiously, there being no good reason to suppose that the operator of the airfoil and my assailant were one and the same. I found where he had lain for the first shot, had knelt for the second, and stood for the third. I did not find any casings; evidently he had policed them up prior to departure. The thicker grass back of the bluffs where the airfoil had been docked was already beginning to pop back up into place under the hot afternoon sun.

Down on the beach, several people had clustered around something on the sand. I ducked back from the edge of the escarpment before anyone spotted me, then made my way back down to my chair.

The cluster had grown by the time I gathered up the tin of cheroots and the pocket flask of Knockando. One of the young men I had been eyeing earlier turned and pointed in my direction, and said something to a woman standing beside him. Neither seemed pleased, though I had no idea who they thought I was. They stepped aside as I drew near, and revealed what I had already known I would find.

The man on the sand looked to be in his early forties. The white lower legs that protruded from his amply-filled shorts and the pale and rather flabby arms exposed by his undershirt bespoke a lack of familiarity with sunlight. The spreading crimson stain over his left chest stood out in sharp contrast. There was no need to check for a pulse, but I did step forward for a closer look at his face. It was round and slack. His eyes were closed, or had been closed for him, and his skin was clean-shaven. He might have had his nose bobbed. There seemed to be more hair in his black eyebrows than on the rest of his head.

"Who is he?" a young man asked, looking up at me. "Do you know him?"

I started to reply that I had never seen him before in my life, and stopped when I realized that that was not quite true. I had seen this face somewhere, but not recently, and not in association with my work. I felt I should know him. "Has anyone checked for ID?" I asked.

A couple of people edged back. A woman opposite me said, "I'm not touching him."

"I've commoed the constabulary," said the young man who had first addressed me with questions. "They're sending someone."

As if in confirmation of this announcement, a powder blue airfoil arrived at the beach, an amber light flashing on top of its forward

9

cowling. It settled onto the sand some ten meters away, and a young man in a green and brown uniform dismounted smartly. His patent leather harness supported a sidearm, a charge pouch, a clip for restraints, and an electrical apparatus for stunning miscreants. Although they seemed to be the standard accouterments of his profession, he walked as if he were quite proud of them. My height gave me no chance at all to avoid eventual attention, but I stood well back and hoped to be taken for a curious passer-by. The cluster parted for him. He looked the body over, spoke briefly into his PHL--Personal Holographic Link, to you--and finally identified himself to those around him as Associate Constable Munro. Evidently the Sayoun constabulary was not about to regard seriously a summons from an itinerant beachcomber until the reported crime had been confirmed by sighting. Munro then asked if anyone had seen anything, which seemed to me to be rather an open question, and after a brief silence the woman who had stepped aside at my approach pointed directly at me.

"She has a weapon," she said, "and she was up there on the ridge."

Associate Constable Munro reacted to this revelation by unsnapping his holster, drawing what appeared to be a Kellogg-Feuer of recent manufacture, and aiming it in my direction. This process took him approximately five seconds, the last four and a half of which, as far as I was concerned, were borrowed time. I mean, with the Kellogg so relatively inaccessible, he had no chance whatsoever against a pro. Fortunately for him, Deven asks that his operatives avoid vexing local enforcement officials, insofar as that is possible.

Accordingly, I raised my hands a little and gave Munro my best puzzled smile. He marched forward, and bade me by a gesture with the Kellogg to turn around. When I did so, he pushed me roughly toward the airfoil, adding more borrowed time to his already precarious existence. Evidently he was blissfully unaware that the whole purpose of the Kellogg was to enable him to stand well away from a malefactor and issue instructions to be obeyed or to defend himself to the extreme if necessary. It's only in the entertainment 'grams that the arresting official and the criminal come in close proximity to one another. Put another way, if I am within arm's reach of him, he is within arm's reach of me, and there are about two dozen different maneuvers I can think of that would leave him crippled, maimed, or speaking in a voice pitched high enough to throw bats off-course. To say nothing of dead.

With a scowl from Deven fixed in my mind, I let Munro live while he ushered me to the airfoil. By this time the audience had eased away from the body on the sand and was grouping into twos and threes to observe the final stages of the detention and resolution. Even if Deven allowed us to hold grudges, I bore no ill will toward the woman who had singled me out. Munro, however, was beginning to build up an equity. At his direction I placed my hands on the cowling and stood with my legs apart, while he began a cautious search, locating the Krupp-Stern almost at once. With the weapon confiscated, he patted me down, almost shyly at first. Then, perhaps emboldened by my cooperative attitude, he conducted a thorough search of my top, discovering that I had concealed there neither a brassiere nor other deadly armaments, before proceeding south to my cut-offs. It would have been simpler to turn the pockets inside-out, but he apparently felt that a slow and careful plumbing of their depths would prove more revelatory. He located my PHL and a set of credentials that, when he flipped them open, meant nothing to him. He also confiscated a fundscard, a handkerchief, the flask, the cheroot tin, and two or three clots of lint. Finally, in order to assure himself of personal security while he transported me back to the constabulary, he tucked my hands to the small of my back and bound the wrists back-to-back with an electronically activated zipstrip. And all the while I consoled myself with mental images of rendering him unable to reproduce. Not that I would fulfill such a desire, of course--in Blacklight Section we disregard petty annoyances--but Deven understands that it's the thought that counts.

Besides, I already had the feeling that there was something more to my visit to Adenne than a mere period of relaxation. The vague familiarity of the face of the dead man was evidence enough of that. All I had to do was make contact with Deven and find out what it was.

A hard shove from Associate Constable Munro brought me back to the present moment. "Board up," he ordered. He waited while I climbed onto the running board and onto the starboard chair, then rounded the stern of the airfoil and fitted himself onto the port chair, his left hand keeping the Kellogg trained on me while he futzed with the controls on the instrumentation console. Presently we were airborne and gliding along the sand and grass toward Sayoun, passing another airfoil along the way, this one white and emblazoned with a universally-understood red cross. Evidently the security of the crime scene was of no particular importance. For me that bode, as they say, ill.

Sayoun passed for civilization on this part of the west coast of the continent known as Equatoria. The commercial aspects of the town dealt primarily with catering to those who came to the area for R&R: cafes, hostels, little shops purveying trinkets and curios, a couple of taverns, an agency that let airfoils and other personal ground conveyances. Street vendors pushed carts and hawked various comestibles, including grilled meats and bread rolls. Many of the structures were of red brick with wood trim, others primarily of timbers and panels. The attendant population dwelt in irregular swatches of residential areas. It comprised retirees from the lower economic strata and young adults who wanted to leave and seek their fortunes but were financially unable to do so. Sayoun was, then, a town of the jaded and disappointed, seasoned now and then with tourists and vacationers who sought for a few days the tranquility of the seacoast.

The constabulary itself was located near the center of Sayoun, as one might expect, but it looked to be nothing more than a wood-and-stone tavern that had been remodeled to support law enforcement. I reckoned that until now the most serious offenses had involved brawling or vandalism.

Associate Constable Munro docked the airfoil in one of the angle slots in front of the constabulary--two other slots were filled, and one more was empty, suggesting a force of four or five on duty at one time-- and ordered me into the building, himself following, this time at a prudent distance, now that my hands were confined. I shouldered the door open and stepped inside.

A partition had been removed to turn the tavern into one continuous bay, illuminated by an array of glow panels that bisected the ceiling's long axis. Along the back wall, in the shadows, stood three chain-link wire cages, none occupied at the moment. Two rows of three small desks each had been spaced along the front wall. There was no receiving clerk in attendance, but at a single, larger desk at the far end of the bay sat a ruddy, burly man in a uniform like Munro's, without the accouterments and with a fringe of gray hair and a face full of experience. He motioned for us to approach the desk, and pointed us to the two wooden chairs in front of it.

The green and brown uniforms were unfamiliar to me. Most security elements in the Amphictyony of Corporations have specific colors for their duty attire, with easily identifiable shoulder patches and insignia of rank. Although Adenne nominally fell under the control of Amphictyony Resources Corporation, the Sayoun constabulary evidently did not. The anomaly was curious, and reminded me that Deven had expressed an unexpected interest when informed of my travel plans.

"Adenne," Deven had repeated three days earlier, sitting at his desk in front of a holographic mood panorama of an orange, rugged mountain range on some obscure world. I preferred the ocean scenes, myself, but this was his office. Dark eyes on his sharp olive face gazed up at me. "Any particular reason, Lieutenant?"

"The travel'grams of the beaches appealed, sir," I said. "Plus it has a low population, it's remote from the Amphictyony, and nobody there cares who I am. I'll only be gone for ten days, sir. I expect Blacklight can do without me for that long." I looked at him sharply. "Unless, of course, you need me for an assignment."

"No, no," he said quickly. "You've accrued considerable vacation time, Lieutenant. Report back in ten days. Oh, and do stop by the Rec Room on your way out."

The Recognition Room housed all available information regarding any potential adversaries an operative might possibly encounter during the course of an assignment or a furlough. A stop in the Rec Room was required of every operative who visited headquarters. A woman who answered only to the name Judra ran the place with the demeanor of a frustrated curmudgeon who had long grown intolerant of specious requests for the best sites for local talent, so to speak. I reported to her desk and told her of my destination, and she sat me before a monitor, called up a few dossiers, and had me review them.

Recalling those reviews now in the open bay, I muttered something vile. The burly man gazed at me across the desk, his thick hands folded neatly on the desk top in front of him. His hologram and dossier had been one of those I had reviewed in the Rec Room. He was regarded as dangerous, but not necessarily adversarial. His name was Frankl Grenke, and at present he seemed to be playing the role of a village constable. Doubtless he was already hand-in-glove with the local power structure, and perhaps had presented himself as someone along the lines of a retired security manager, though to what end, I could not even begin to guess.

"What was that?" he asked. He did not smile, but studied me

thoughtfully after my shrug, as if considering which piece of me to have broken. Finally he turned his pale blue eyes to Munro. "Report," he said.

Associate Constable Munro gave a brief but detailed summary of his actions, omitting a few bits regarding his search of me. I said nothing; other than his identification of the shooter as me, his report was factual enough.

The burly man broke the silence that followed. "Who are you?"

"Who are *you?*" I countered, though I already knew the answer.

His hands did not unfold, but his knuckles whitened a little. "I am Constable Grenke. I won't ask you again."

"My name is Nyx," I said. His expression invited me to tell him the rest of it, but that would never be forthcoming, as I'd been abandoned without surname the evening of my birth. I made a little show of cooperation. "I work for AmResCor Ways & Means. Your associate constable here took my credentials and several other items into custody, the better to protect them from pilfering."

The blood returned to Grenke's fingers. "And why did you kill the man on the beach?"

"I never saw him," I replied, and gave him an abbreviated version of events. "I've not yet been informed of the reason for my detention," I finished.

Grenke looked to Munro, who placed my Krupp-Stern on the desk. "She was carrying this," he reminded the constable. "And the killer always returns to the scene of the crime."

I nodded toward the Stern. "That's an energy weapon," I said patiently. "Even a superficial forensic examination will show that the victim was killed by a bullet fired from a high-powered rifle."

"And you can prove this, I suppose," said Grenke.

I put a snarl into my voice. "Come off it, Constable. I don't have to prove squat. Your own medics will confirm my statement. As for returning to the scene of the crime, I was returning to my chair when I noticed the small crowd. I was curious. I had assumed the man with the rifle was shooting at me."

Grenke appeared to consider this. "Why would anyone shoot at you, *M'selle* Nyx?"

I was making progress, having been promoted to the standard French honorific. "I couldn't even begin to answer that question, Constable." I gave him a count of five, and added, "Has anyone checked on a scarlet and gold airfoil that probably arrived in Sayoun maybe ten minutes before we did?"

"You think the killer is in Sayoun?"

I shrugged. "He was headed this way, the last I saw."

Grenke reached a decision, and his expression said I was not going to like it. "We're going to hold you here, pending further investigation," he told me. "Even if your story checks out, you're a material witness."

I made a face and nodded, all the while deliberately drawing several rapid and shallow breaths. Finally I rose from the chair, felt the onset of planned dizziness as the blood drained from my face, and collapsed onto the floor, bending myself into a hairpin at the hips. Long legs can be a bit of a curse at times, but interminable hours of agility training had enabled me to tuck my butt through the loop of my arms and then draw them along my legs until they were free, or at least in front of me. Grenke and Munro had two seconds in which to react, and neither made it. Mouth agape, Munro was staring at me; Grenke seemed to realize that something was amiss, and was reaching for his weapon. In the third second I rose to my knees, snagged the Stern from the desk, and trained it on them. Belated protests from tendons in the backs of my knees made me wince while I scrambled back to my feet.

Munro's face now wore a stricken look. "You can't get away with this," he yammered.

The desk had blocked Grenke's view of me while I freed myself during the contrived fainting spell, but he had managed to stand up. Now he sat back down, wary eyes not on the Stern, but on me. Well, that figured. Grenke was enough of a pro to know that incipient weapons fire always begins in the eyes.

"I have nothing to get away with," I said quietly, and placed the Stern back on the desk. "And I have no reason to mislead you, or to lie."

Munro winkled his Kellogg out and held it on me. "Don't move!"

He still had not learned that a sidearm is most effective when it is out of reach of the target. A simple sweep of my arm timed with a snap-kick would have left him with a voice that could cause dolphins to beach themselves, if the oceans of Adenne had dolphins. I sighed, and looked down at Grenke. "You couldn't possibly have trained him," I said. "Your forehead would be flat, and there would be indentations in the walls here."

"I suppose you think returning your weapon should make us believe you," said Grenke.

"That would be one way." I held my hands up, and he withdrew his PHL, set a code, and passed it over the zipstrip, which fell open. Rubbing my wrists to increase circulation, I gave Munro a long look. "You left my other items in the airfoil," I said at last. "Please go and get them."

Grenke nodded assent.

If you can do it, you can damn well look at it. Deven has little regard for operatives who cannot bear to see the results of their handiwork. I watched Munro as he strode to the door and threw it open, and watched as he spilled backwards onto the floor of the open bay, spread-eagled and deader than field rations.

002

I heard Grenke hit the floor behind me, but no report from the bullet that had been fired at Munro. Probably the shot had been made from directly across the street. Staying below the tops of the desks for cover, I crept forward until I was just within reach of Munro's body. Two fingers on his wrist denied the existence of a pulse. I glanced over my shoulder and shook my head at Grenke, who had crawled round his desk. Peering under the desk yielded a clear view of the open doorway, which gave onto the street and the outdoor cafe on the other side. There, several patrons relaxed on the boardwalk, oblivious to all but their beverages and conversations. On either side of the cafe stood kiosks, one for trinkets, the other purveying small packages of comestibles. Given that Munro had plunged straight back into the bay, it seemed likely that the shooter had positioned himself between the cafe and one of the kiosks, but all I saw there now was shrubbery.

Grenke had already regained his feet, and spoke briefly into the PHL. I eased back behind a desk to await developments. Seconds later an airfoil came to a stop directly in front of the doorway. I risked a peek around the corner of the desk and saw that the craft's operator was wearing a constabulary uniform. Grenke extended a hand and helped me to my feet.

"Frazier says it's clear now." He paused, and gave me a hard look.

"You *knew* someone was out there, yet you sent Munro to his death."

"Better him than me. And no, I didn't know, not for sure. Now, I know."

Grenke started to reply, then changed his mind. I could see in his blue eyes a coldness that conceded that I had acted professionally, and given his deep background he would understand that. But no commander likes to lose personnel unnecessarily. Munro's death had served to liberate me from suspicion regarding the killing on the beach, but perhaps at the cost of local cooperation. Well, that was Grenke's problem, not mine. I hadn't been ordered to gain anyone's cooperation. I had in fact no orders whatsoever, yet. But I didn't think they'd be long in coming.

The airfoil operator entered the bay. His uniform bore the same insignia of rank as Munro's. Through the doorway behind him I spotted two more airfoils arrive and dock, their operators dismounting. Grenke leaned closer to me and whispered conspiratorially, "You're not Ways & Means. One of the corporate security units, maybe? Perhaps AmSec?"

"I think the crisis has passed for now," I said, and gave him my PHL code. "I've told you everything I know about this, but if you have more questions for me, ask. I'm staying at *The Silver Pestle*. If I'm not there, I'll be on the beach."

Grenke drummed his fingers. His expression said that he was not about to write off the murder of one of his personnel, even if his only suspect could account for herself. He could accept that I did not kill Munro, but if I didn't, who did? And did I know who did? Finally he addressed Associate Constable Frazier with his decision, "Transport her to the *Pestle*, then report back here."

I accepted the offer. Deven was going to give me a goddamn commendation, what with all the cooperation I had demonstrated. I wondered what else he would have to say.

Frazier, for all his trappings of local security, proved to be an unassuming young man who went about his business as he was told, without posing or fanfare. We boarded up the airfoil, and he raised it smoothly and peeled back onto the street and toward the east without raising a dust cloud on the cobblestone street. In other attire he might have passed for a chauffeur. He stood about ten centimeters shorter and outdid me by maybe a kilogram, but his most outstanding feature was a studied regard for his surroundings. If he was aware of me as anything more than an order by Grenke to be carried out, he did not let on. His deep blue eyes were keened to dangers on our periphery even while he focused on our destination. His weapons clip was unsnapped, probably against regulations, and almost certainly as a precaution. I reckoned he might actually be able to extract the weapon in time to be useful, should the need arise.

We turned right, or south, at a corner market, where the locals bought fresh produce, herbs, seasonings, grains, fish, and poultry. The heat of the day had waned, but the aromas remained, and reminded me that I had consumed nothing since breakfast except half the contents of the flask. The lower level of *The Silver Pestle* was devoted to a bar and a deli, and I started to make a mental note for dinner when Frazier said something to me that absolutely did not register.

Asked to repeat it, he said, "At this market they'll have recipes as well."

"Sorry. Was I drooling?"

He kept his eyes on the street, but managed a grin. "Not noticeably. It takes a while to prepare, but *sahjita* chicken is a local dish, if a bit piquant. That yellow powder in one of the bins yields the cooking sauce."

"I'm better at consuming fine cuisine than preparing it. There's a deli in the *Pestle.*"

"A pity for your palate, that is. Ah, this is you."

Frazier docked the airfoil in front of the inn. I gathered up my effects and dismounted, and waved to him without looking back as I climbed the three steps to the boardwalk that fronted the *Pestle*, and stepped through the open entrance. Under other circumstances I might have looked back and even more, but my furlough had ended the moment that spray of sand had burst up on the beach. I crossed the bar and took the stairs two at a time to the next level and my room directly above the inn's front entrance.

Even on furlough I was normally careful about room security, but the assault on the beach forced me to regard Adenne as hostile territory. Operational protocol now demanded that I enter my own room in the prescribed manner. The telltale I'd left over the sensor pad on the wall-- one of my hairs, yellow and difficult to detect--was still in place. Door security yielded to my right thumb on the pad. I thrust the door open and rolled to one knee, with the Stern sweeping the room. It was empty, and showed no immediate signs of having been searched. My travel bag, placed on the bed in a seemingly casual but precise angle to the foot of the bed, had not been moved. The hygiene alcove, visible from where I knelt, was empty except for the shower, which I rose and cautiously checked. As I did so, the hair on the back of my neck began to prickle, and a spot between my shoulder blades chilled.

Training inculcates habit. If you always do the same thing in a given situation, over and over, then you never have to ask yourself whether you did it this time. On a shelf under the mirror above the wash basin rested my toothbrush. After I had used it this morning, I had left it, as always, on its back, brush to the right, parallel to the edge of the shelf. It now lay at a slight angle to the edge. A seismic quake might have displaced the toothbrush. So might a visit from housekeeping--but maid service would have disturbed much more than just the toothbrush, and in any case I hadn't requested maid service today.

I opened the little plastic container for a bar of bath soap in the shower's soap well. This morning I had placed two folded AV100 notes in it. They were missing, presumed taken. An amateur or a stupid thief would have taken both; a slightly smarter thief would have taken just one, hoping that I would wonder whether I had miscounted. And a pro would have left both in order to protect his surreptitious entry, or he would have taken both as a ruse, to mislead me into thinking a stupid thief or amateur had taken them. The toothbrush, then, and not the missing money, was the clincher. Whoever had searched my room had been very careful and very thorough.

With the PHL set to scan, I checked the room for electronic and photonic surveillance devices, and found nothing. I searched the furniture and travel bag for items that did not belong, and again found nothing. Whoever had tumbled the room appeared to have been interested in acquiring information, not in destroying it.

I changed clothes--to a loose indigo jersey and black cutoffs, if it matters--then sat down on the bed and raised Deven.

There's a rumor that he never sleeps. It may be true: I've never failed to raise him when I needed him, and he has never sounded as if he had just awakened to my signal. I set the PHL to project him life-size onto the floor in the center of the room.

"Bored already, Lieutenant?" he asked. He was sitting placidly at his desk, the mood panorama behind him now a meadow scene. His expression told me nothing. He may have been trying for irony; if so, it was a first.

I brought him up to date on the events that had transpired, from the shots on the beach to Grenke's interrogation. Blacklight operatives do not, you understand, go running to Deven every time someone tries to kill us. We are, however, expected to discourage the practice.

"So you might want to dispatch an operative to Adenne, sir, to deal with this," I finished.

He gave me a stern look. "Don't be coy, Lieutenant."

"No, sir. But golly, sir, I'm on furlough, sir, as you know. Sir."

"Indeed. The victim on the beach was Marvon Terreme. Probably you saw him in a news'gram. Terreme was the deputy manager of the E&E Division of Amphictyony Resources Corporation, and was a favorite target, at least as far as fruits and vegetables are concerned, of Ecotect."

Deven having identified the man from the sketchy description I had given him, I said, "You knew he was here on Adenne, sir."

"It hardly mattered, as you were there on furlough, and Terreme was present on Adenne in a clandestine capacity."

"Pulling Exploration & Exploitation duties, I suppose?"

"Just so. AmResCor will replace him, and send that replacement to Adenne. Your assignment, Lieutenant, is to protect Terreme's replacement by identifying and removing those responsible for killing Terreme, with the limitation that you confine your activities to Adenne."

I made a face at the hologram. "If Ecotect is responsible for the order against Terreme, someone in their hierarchy, off-Adenne, issued it."

"We have been tasked with a specific intervention. It is felt that the response I have ordered will send the message to Ecotect that they are to confine their missiles to produce."

"Ecotect will simply send someone else," I pointed out.

Deven gave me a bleak look. "As much has already been pointed out to those who asked for us. We have been advised that such an eventuality is irrelevant to your orders."

Irrelevant and Need To Know are the two gremlins of an operative's duties. They're each another way of saying, Kill this person, but don't kill him too dead, and mind the bystanders. Occasionally Deven has to tolerate such inane conditions, but unless an operative has been ordered into circumstances that demand his death, Deven prefers that we remain alive. If that means the removal of someone who is irrelevant to our orders and whose identity we do not need to know, that's too bad.

"Understood, sir," I said. "I'll need some background on Ecotect. I know hardly anything about the organization, except that it tries to preserve ecologies and that its members are generally a nuisance."

"It has already been uploaded to Niobe," said Deven. "I'll advise you of the identity of Terreme's replacement as soon as we have it. Report on schedule, Lieutenant."

After the hologram vanished, I raised Niobe, the 'skipcomp aboard my spaceskip, the *Kuremsha*, and read the Ecotect file. As background it was informative but not useful. Well, I hadn't expected it to be. I was dealing with a pro here on Adenne, possibly more than one, and Ecotect was not known to have connections to that type of resource. Something about the organization had changed.

The origins of Ecotect are shrouded back in the times when humanity still had not left Earth. There were diverse, disparate units that worked to save endangered species of flora and fauna, encourage waste recycling, that sort of thing. After humanity left Earth for other worlds, the ancestors of Ecotect expanded their concerns to include those worlds, but the vast distances of interstellar space made it impossible for separate units to police human settlements. In time, and after much infighting and acrimony, The Ecology Protective Association, or TEPA, was born. Almost immediately it was pointed out that a unit with a remarkably similar acronym had been responsible for much of the infighting, and, after more acrimony, the compromise appellation Ecology Protection, or Ecotect, was adopted.

Soon Ecotect was ubiquitous. Volunteers were dispatched to disrupt exploration, settlement, and exploitation, to such an extent that corporate security personnel were assigned to prevent said volunteers from such disruptions. Inasmuch as the volunteers were armed with bananas and squash and the security personnel with energy weapons, disruptions were soon reduced to anomalies. Every now and then, someone scored a success, and a corporate hierarch was doused with rotten peaches, whipped cream, gooey lettuce, and harsh language. None of this should have been of the slightest interest to Blacklight.

But now Terreme was dead, presumably at the hands of a professional assassin, a mortifice, contracted by Ecotect. Technically it was still a matter for corporate security to resolve, or perhaps Amphictyony Security, but Blacklight had been tasked with the resolution, and now so had I. Mine not to reason why, and so forth.

I considered my leads: a dead man on the beach; another in the constabulary; an elusive assassin armed with a rifle; the involvement of Ecotect; the search of my room in the inn; and Constable Grenke, whose dossier had been among those I had seen in the Rec Room just prior to my departure on furlough.

The pale red sun had reached the horizon, and the entire sky seemed to be shutting down. Outside the window, shadows poured onto the street like syrup. Yellow fusion globes on poles soon began to glow, revealing movements of people as the night life of Sayoun commenced. Most of them looked like tourists, heading toward the restaurants for dinner. I was mulling over joining them when someone knocked on my door.

It seemed unlikely that a malefactor, intent on harm, would announce his presence, but I was no longer on furlough. I took up the prescribed position and instructed the visitor to enter. I had no idea whom to expect, but way down on my list would have been Frazier, bearing a covered dinner tray. I tucked the Stern under my belt and bade him step further into the room.

Associate Constable Frazier had shed his uniform since going off-duty, and now wore something almost touristy, black denims and a light jersey that enhanced the ultramarine of his eyes. He'd given his short brown hair a crisp brushing and otherwise made himself presentable, his erect bearing the only remnant of his official persona. At my behest he placed the tray on the writing table by the window and drew the white cloth from it. The tray contained a silver charger of roast chicken liberally doused with a rich yellow sauce, a silver gravy boat containing more sauce, and a pair of brown ceramic tureens, one of vegetable broth, the other filled with some dish made from chopped eggs and cheese. The cloth removed, the room began to fill with the aromas of the food, and reminded me that I'd had nothing to eat since a couple of bagels and cream cheese for breakfast.

"So you cook, too," I said.

"'Too?'"

I picked up the knife and fork he had provided and prodded the chicken. "In addition to keeping order in Sayoun and coming to rescue me at the constabulary."

A smile touched his eyes and almost made it to his mouth. "I doubt someone like you requires a lot of rescuing, *M'selle* Nyx."

It was difficult to manage a, "Someone like me?" with my mouth full, but I got most of it out. Frazier had been right--*sahjita* chicken was abundantly piquant. Already beads of sweat had popped out on my forehead. I tried to blunt the taste with a sip of broth, and restored my voice. "And you can cancel the honorific," I added. "It's just Nyx."

Frazier nodded toward the tray. "How is it?"

"Incendiary."

"Welcome to Adenne."

I sat down at the table and made several more incisions, reducing the split breast to mere mouthfuls, while Frazier, after some hesitation, docked himself on the edge of the bed, seated at attention, and watched. Apparently the broth was intended to take the bite off the sauce, and I alternated between it and the meat, thus comforting most of my taste buds. The sauce itself was smooth and rather like vindaloo. But I had not come to Adenne to investigate culinary delights.

"Someone like me?" I repeated, as I started on the other tureen.

"Constable Grenke speculated that you are far more acquainted with security protocols than with ways and means," answered Frazier. "He briefed me accordingly after I returned to the constabulary. By the way, we found where the shooter was kneeling when he killed Associate Constable Munro."

"Beside the cafe?"

"The shrubbery there provided sufficient concealment, though of course it was worthless as cover. We're checking transportation outlets for the airfoil you described. Someone let it to the killer. We'll find it."

The egg and cheese pudding finished, I said, "You won't find anything to trace."

Frazier nodded. "I suspect you are correct. But that's a curious assessment, coming from someone from Ways & Means."

"Have you identified the victim on the beach?" Frazier shook his head, and I went on, "Marvon Terreme, head of E&E, AmResCor. He may or may not have signed in at a stay-the-night under that name. If he left a 'skip at the Spaceport, it might not be registered in his name."

Frazier scowled. "You're not Nyx from Ways & Means."

"My name *is* Nyx. The information I just gave you came from my boss. He did not specify that the constabulary should not have it. If you need to use your PHL to convey it, I'll wait."

23

He shook his head. "There's no point in pursuing the investigation this late in the evening. Are you done with that?"

"Burp."

"Would you care to take a brief tour of Sayoun?"

"Dinner and a stroll. That's a promising start to the evening." I piled the dishes and utensils onto the tray and covered it. "Yes, I'd love a tour. Or are you also hoping for an opportunity to use that handweapon tucked against the small of your back?"

Frazier looked chagrined. "I wondered whether you had noticed. Ways and Means, indeed."

I stood up, and pulled up the front of my jersey to reveal the Krupp-Stern and a bit more. "Let's go."

Frazier opened the door, and closed it behind us. He had the presence of mind to go on down the stairs so that I might emplace my telltale, another hair over the wall sensor pad, in private. I still wondered what I had done to deserve his attention. Perhaps he was merely following orders from Grenke. If so, I'd have to have a word about that with the Constable in the morning.

Nighttime Sayoun had all the bustle of an R&R town. Clusters of vacationers and tourists wove their way along the boardwalks, while the locals kept to themselves, eyes wary and defensive, as they hunched over refreshments at outdoor cafes. As with any festive grouping, a brawl was a possibility, but the travel'grams had assured me that the town deserved its reputation as a haven for those seeking peace and quiet. Score another victory for promotion over accuracy and quality.

Frazier led me down a dimly-lit sideway toward a tavern away from the festivities. Along the way we passed kiosks that purveyed tobaccos, candies, designed stimulants, and small vials of liquors, and alcoves of shrubbery that sheltered benches for those who wished to sit and talk. Frazier's tense demeanor suggested that at any moment a miscreant armed with a silenced rifle might take a shot at us from some dark nook. He had already inferred that someone like me probably did not require a lot of rescuing or protection, which meant he might be thinking along the same lines I was: although I had been present during the shootings, others in my vicinity had been the targets. And Frazier was now in my vicinity. Either he was brave, or foolhardy, or one of us was overthinking this.

We reached the tavern--*The Bantam Cock*, an appellation doubtless bestowed by a dissatisfied female patron--without incident. Upon entry we drew one or two speculative looks, but nothing untoward. Someone at one of the far tables waved and called to Frazier, and he acknowledged the greeting with a jerk of his head as we approached the bar. Frazier beckoned to the keep and ordered two mugs of ale, put them on a tab when they arrived, and escorted them and me to a corner booth occupied by a couple with whom he seemed acquainted, although he might have chosen the booth because it afforded a full view of the interior of the tavern and left our backs to the wall. The man had a beach tan amply displayed by his brown jersey with the sleeves torn off, and a physique that might prove useful in the event it became necessary to repeatedly lift chunks of iron, but it was the woman who snagged my attention. She was dressed unremarkably enough--much as I was, in fact, though her pullover was the same gray as her eyes. I had no idea yet what name she went by here on Adenne, but her dossier in the Rec Room belonged to a highly skilled and expensive freelance killer, or mortifice, named Silver LeMay.

003

Anyone who knows what to look for can see through the various façades and beguilements of my profession. Attire is irrelevant, and most of the time so is posture and body language. But the eyes almost never lie. Not even tinted lenses can conceal that nebula behind the irises that identifies those whose job it is to remove someone from a situational equation. Though I cannot see it in a mirror, I've been told I have that cloudiness. It's more prominent when the eyes are narrowed and alert to danger. LeMay's eyes were slits as she watched me draw up to the L-shaped booth.

There was, I was pleased to note, no question of priority in seating. Frazier slid in first, which left me with the outside position in the event I had to move quickly. I wondered whether he regarded me as, between us, the more skilled in self-defense. Of course, in our line of work, self-defense is not quite the preferred approach, as our orders generally insist upon pre-emptive lethal action. I wondered, too, how much of Frazier's behavior resulted from his estimate of our respective capabilities, and how much was based on information given him by Constable Grenke, who in our Rec Room files was known as Grenke the Glacier, the nickname referring to his slow and grinding methods of attaining his personal and professional aims.

Grenke, however, was not here. I listened while Frazier made introductions. The wad of muscle answered to Thone. His handshake was not merely firm; he was a crusher, and I escaped having my carpals bundled by shoving my hand far into his, so that he had to be content with working on my wrist. He abandoned this effort as Frazier indicated LeMay, sitting as I was on the outside, but on the opposite leg of the L.

"Diana, Nyx," he said. "Nyx, Diana."

We, too, shook hands, a brief and harmless clasping. I gave her a little prod, to see how she would react. "As I recall, in mythology, Diana was a huntress."

LeMay inclined her head in acknowledgement. "And Nyx was the Goddess of Night," she said pleasantly, her gray eyes only slightly narrowed, and with just a hint of mirth in them. "However, there is no game in here, and these walls shield us from the darkness."

The message to me was clear: everyone was safe in here as long as I behaved myself. I selected one of the mugs Frazier had brought and gave her a little toast in acceptance. I didn't believe it for a second, of course, and neither did LeMay. She'd do what she thought she had to do, as would I, regardless of non-verbal assurances to the contrary. I wondered what she had to do here in *The Bantam Cock*, but discretion overrode any direct questions I might have. If I wanted information from her here, I'd have to approach from the flank.

The dossier listed Silver LeMay as a meter seventy-seven and sixty-eight kilos, and I saw nothing to suggest she had added or subtracted anything. The holograms on file showed her with different hair lengths and colors, but what they used to call platinum, its present color, seemed to be natural to her. She was proficient with all sorts of weaponry, including rifles and pistols, but preferred the Ecko line of energy handweapons, and was reported to have used an Ecko 507, the model number indicating the year of manufacture, to fulfill a contract on Skadany, and probably had not yet upgraded from last year. Her history suggested that she knew some unarmed combat moves, but generally hired local talent for the heavy lifting--in this instance, Thone, which explained the disparity between his tan and hers.

Professionally, I knew her by sight and by specifics of the dossier, but as we had never encountered one another previously in the field, she could only reckon that I was in her general line of work. This gave me just enough advantage to press her. Accordingly, I downed a gulp of ale and asked, "How's your R&R going?"

"I start my tan tomorrow."

"Maybe I'll see you on the beach again."

Bemused, she said, "Again?"

I gave her a thoughtful look, and shook my head. "Sorry. I thought I might have seen you down there this afternoon."

She signaled the keep for a refill. "I was busily checking in at *The Silver Pestle* this afternoon," she said, and she did not even crack a smile at the name.

"That's where Nyx is staying," said Frazier.

Now LeMay broke a wide smile. "Is it? Maybe I'll see you in the deli for breakfast tomorrow." The refill arrived, and she added, "Assuming I'm sober by then."

"So how did you and Frazier meet?" I asked her.

"We have some common interests," said LeMay. A wave of understanding lightened her eyes, and she added, "Oh, I see what you're asking. I've been here in Sayoun now for two days. I stayed aboard my *Zoraya*, finishing up some business, and getting out at night," here she glanced at Frazier, "and met him. How about you?"

I hedged the truth. "He wanted to ask me some questions about a killing on the beach," I said, watching her carefully.

"A killing?" LeMay cried. "That's terrible! What happened? Who was it?"

"We're still not sure," said Frazier. "Anyway, there's nothing to be done about it right now, which is why we're all here, right?" He raised his mug. "To summer, and Adenne."

Even Thone agreed with that one. "Is this your vacation, too?" I asked him.

He shook his head. LeMay said, "He works in Shipments, out at the Spaceport." She looked at him and added, pointedly, "You said you had an early shift tomorrow."

Thone's heavy brow knit, and he started to speak, then thought better of it, and stood up to leave. Rather than allow him to pass in front of her, thus blocking her view of me, LeMay rose also and let him ease behind her. "See you tomorrow," he said, and left the tavern.

I shot a look at Frazier. He seemed oblivious to the intricate byplay. LeMay resumed her seat, a wry smile more in her eyes than on her lips. Someone hailed Frazier from across the tavern. Out of the corner of my eye I saw him turn and wave. LeMay nodded, as if to herself in confirmation of something, and leaned on the table top, folding her arms there, her hands in plain view. Frazier mumbled excuses and rose, and I slid from the bench and allowed him to pass behind me. He said something about catching me up later. LeMay, meanwhile, had not moved, though her gaze transfixed me. Stay or go, she seemed to be asking, but the deliberate vulnerability of her position at the table was an invitation for me to remain.

I sat back down, hands now clasped together on the table. For long seconds we eyed one another. I had no idea how LeMay expected the encounter to evolve, but between us any cover stories we might have emplaced were blown already. We two alone knew who--or more precisely, what--we were, but that information need not pass on to anyone else.

I hoisted my mug in another toast, this one silent. After a long pull, LeMay set hers down carefully, and her finger began to trace a design in the condensation on the table. Finally she said, "I like to watch nature holograms in my spare time. Animals hunting interest me, as you might imagine. Did you know lions from the same pride often cooperate to make a kill?"

"I believe it's the lionesses that do most of the hunting," I said.

"Yes, of course. Lionesses." She studied the design she had traced. "I don't know you," she went on. "I can tell you know me. As we have never met, you must therefore have seen a file, a dossier. That suggests you have official sanction." Here she paused, and looked up at me. "I gather I am not your primary target?"

"I don't know."

So help me, she chuckled. "Don't you just hate that kind of assignment?"

I shrugged. "They don't crop up often."

"Are you done with that?" she asked, pointing to the mug.

"Why?"

LeMay looked around. "We're two women sitting together, more or less. Either we're looking for company, or we're here with each other. Sooner or later, someone is going to try to find out which. We can avoid that unpleasantness by leaving. Unless you and he . . . " She left the sentence unfinished.

I did not take my eyes off her to glance in Frazier's direction. "I came to Adenne for R&R, Diana," I said. "That's the truth. I just want to drink whiskey, smoke cheroots, and so forth."

"Ah, yes," she said archly. "'And so forth.'"

"What about you?"

"Thone isn't my type for 'so forth,'" she said. "He's default. If there's a problem, he handles it, so I don't have to blow my cover except by choice . . . or as circumstances indicate. Cards on the table?"

I shook my head. "I may not be able to reciprocate."

She leaned closer and whispered, "I'm Silver LeMay. That confirms what I know you already know. Diana is my 'skipcomp, incidentally."

"I'm still Nyx."

LeMay got up, and offered me a hand. When I hesitated, she said, "For the reasons I just gave you, we ought to head back to the *Pestle*."

I declined the hand, but climbed to my feet and moved just out of her reach. "There's something I probably should tell you," I said, as we stepped toward the door.

"What's that? You're strictly Frazier-type?"

"In fact, regarding 'so forth,' I'm omnivorous. No, that's not it."

A cautious smile tickled the corners of her mouth. "Same here. So what then?"

We emerged back into the night, and she turned around to face me, waiting. "I may not be safe to be around," I told her. "I've been shot at today."

"Yes, I know."

"You?"

She turned away, expecting me to follow. I did so, fingers curled around the butt of the Stern under my jersey. She did not respond, but continued walking at a good pace up the side street and toward the *Pestle*. "Silver?" I called, several steps behind her.

She stopped, and waited for me to catch her up. "You have to regard anything I tell you as not necessarily true," she said softly. "I understand. I have to view your statements in the same way. For what it's worth, I

29

did not shoot at you, nor do I know who did. And please call me Diana."

In silence we resumed our stroll, reaching the main street to turn right. Only a few lights remained on in *The Silver Pestle,* and those mostly on the first level and its bar. On either side of the street every other fusion globe had been extinguished for the night, and the clots of people I had seen earlier had by now found shelter, at least until closing time. Out in the open, we were certainly vulnerable to a sniper, even at night. Senses keened, I was prepared to duck, draw, and fire as we made our way along the boardwalk. But nothing happened, and if LeMay was aware of my tension, she did not let on, although she seemed to make a point of keeping me to her left, presumably to free her right hand for weaponry. By the time we reached the inn, I had begun to relax, ever so slightly.

The deli had closed for the evening, and the bar held only a couple of patrons and appeared on the verge of pulling the curtains. LeMay and I took the stairs to the second level. Almost immediately after we reached the landing she said, "This is me."

I made a little gesture. "I'm three doors down."

"I know." She stood at the door, looking uncomfortable. "Nyx, I . . . have to confer with my principals. It might take a while."

"I have a similar task," I told her. "If you don't mind, I'd like to wait here until your door snicks shut."

LeMay tucked her long hair under the neck of her pullover to get it out of the way. "I have to go in rough," she said, and grimaced. "Well, you know that."

"Do you want me to stay and cover you?"

She shook her head. "My door and sensor pad fail-safes are still secure," she said. "But if you're going to watch, the room layout forces me to tuck and roll to the right."

LeMay did not have my training, but the entry procedure she followed was one of the options also available to me. Nothing sizzled or popped at her when she opened the door and blew inside. The lights brightened at her voice command, and she seemed to be alone. After another minute of searching, she gave me a high sign and closed the door, slowly, to the *snick.*

I moved down the hallway, wondering if I should have stayed with LeMay. True, she probably had to wait for a while to reach some or all of her principals, however many they might be, but there are things that can be done while waiting, and I was definitely in a mood for some of them, even though I had to report to Deven as soon as I finished checking my own room. The hair on the sensor pad was still reassuringly in place, but on the latch side of the door, the gap between it and the jamb appeared wider by two or three millimeters.

It seemed unlikely that a miscreant had returned to the room to search it again in the hope of finding some more currency. More probably, he had left something behind intended for me, and I doubted it was flowers or a fruit basket. Cautiously I knelt down to examine the gap more closely, and caught a whiff of bananas. A return visit to Silver LeMay seemed indicated.

The procedure for approaching a room inhabited by a killer is much the same as that for opening the door to one's own room, with a couple of differences, the most important being that the operative does not actually mean to enter. I stood to one side--in theory, it doesn't matter which--and rapped sharply on her door. Moments later I heard a muffled, "Who is it?"

LeMay was probably speaking through a towel or curtain to help disguise her location within, and make it sound like she might be as far away as the opposite wall or the hygiene alcove. I reckoned her within two meters of the door, weapon out. "The Goddess of Night," I said.

"Stand in front of the door," she said, still muffled. "You know the drill."

I did so, and waited, hands visible and empty. Even so, it took her longer than I expected to respond. When at last she threw open the door, I had a clear view of her room but none of her, although the clothing she had been wearing lay in a pile on the floor, off to my right. Still following procedure, she dipped her head carefully to peer past the jamb from well inside the room. Satisfied, she stepped fully into view.

She was wearing a dull pink sleep shirt that fell limply to mid-thigh, and with the fusion globe directly behind her, very clearly nothing else except a length of rope or something very like it looped around her hips under the shirt, and from which dangled her Ecko 507 by her thigh. I reckoned she had changed clothes directly she had learned the identity of her caller, and taken up a position calculated for effect.

I said, "I'd like to borrow a liter of water."

LeMay actually laughed, a full-throated burst that totally belied the perils inherent in our encounter. Then she sobered, and lines of genuine concern creased her brow. "What's wrong?"

"A few sheets of paper would be nice," I added. "Or something relatively water-resistant that I can roll up."

"Nyx---"

I allowed myself a momentary weakness--it wasn't difficult to do, given her present attire--and made a mental note not to include it in my after-action report, assuming I survived the action. "The offer is nice, Diana," I told her, "but the timing is really bad."

Her expression said that we shared the same weakness. She made one more attempt. "Won't this keep till morning?"

"They have maid service here. I don't want maid fragments all over my room."

Quickly she retrieved her shorts and climbed back into them, keeping the loop and Ecko outside them and under her sleep shirt. She glanced up at me as she fastened the shorts. "Scritchy?" she asked.

"That's my guess. What do you have?"

"Water's in the fresher, and some courtesy cups." She began rummaging through her travel bag, on the bed. "I don't have any paper. A plastic straw might do, though."

Already I had drawn two cups. "It might, at that," I called. With four full cups in tow, I rejoined her in the room, and we set off for mine, LeMay taking the time to secure her own door behind us.

"Any idea who left it?" LeMay asked, as we reached my door.

"Anyone on Adenne except Frazier, you, and me."

"How do you eliminate me?"

"The Scritchy wasn't there when Frazier and I left," I said, setting the cups down on the floor by the door. "You couldn't have gotten here, broken security, emplaced it, and then beaten us to the tavern."

"It only takes a couple seconds to install," argued LeMay.

I knelt down and peered into the gap. "No, this isn't you," I said. "Pass me that straw."

A Scritchy consists of two small rectangles of flexible latex each smeared on one side with a layer of high explosive that activates when it crystallizes. The explosive surfaces are then arranged so that they are in contact with one another, and with adhesive on the outer surfaces. You can affix the Scritchy to the jamb or to the door. Either way, when the door is pulled shut, the Scritchy adheres to both the jamb and the door. The two rectangles are put together so that the faces of the crystals on one surface oppose those on the other. Thus, when the door is opened, the two surfaces grate against one another--rather like striking a match. Detonation, which occurs almost immediately, destroys the door and jamb with the overall effect of a fragmentation grenade. It's possible to survive it, but most of those who have done wish they hadn't.

Scritchies have one weakness: the manufacturing process of the explosive includes a fixing with isoamyl acetate--the same stuff that gives bananas their distinctive aroma--and thus their presence can be detected. In fact, they have two weaknesses, and Silver LeMay and I were about to address the second.

Aware of what I was about, LeMay had already crimped one end of the straw before handing it to me. I sank that end into one of the water cups, sucked the straw full of water, and capped the top of it, first with my tongue, then with my fingertip. I then inserted the crimped end into the gap above the Scritchy and released the water, a little of which trickled down the outside of the door. "Repeat as needed," I muttered, and did so, until all four cups were empty.

During the ten minutes that had transpired, LeMay had said not a word, but when I finally sat back on my haunches and took a deep, steadying breath, she broke the silence.

"Be sure to push it open slowly," she reminded me.

I nodded. "It should be soggy enough, but step well back, just in case."

LeMay obeyed. "I'll post the remains to Blacklight," she said, "if you'll tell me the address."

"Mind your eyes," I instructed, and nudged the door open.

Insoluble in water, the adhesive held, but the waterlogged layers themselves parted without effect. I pried them loose--the explosive was now a gooey and inert mass-- and tossed them onto the bed. Aware of warmth behind me, I turned around to find LeMay standing just inside the doorway and well within arm's reach. Already taunted by anticipation due to my unexpected return to her room, she was suffering from additional desires brought on by having survived this latest threat to life and limb.

"I still have to report in," I told her, banking my own pangs. "I reckon you still do, too."

The air around her began to cool back to room temperature. "Yes. Yes, of course." She turned to go. "Breakfast in the deli tomorrow?"

"I'd better meet you there," I told her.

"That would be least complicated," she agreed. "Good night."

Alone at last, I raised Deven and made my report. By the time I finished he was frowning, a marked change from the customary stoic reception he gave to reports from the field. "So this Frazier invited you out and then left you there, rather unceremoniously, it would seem," he said. "Have you any idea what was so important that he was willing to sacrifice whatever promise your allures held for him?"

"My wiles hadn't yet come into play, sir. And no, no idea. There were three people at that table the first time I looked in that direction, when we were standing at the bar. Two young men, one woman--a girl, really. I don't have enough to give you useful descriptions. By the time Frazier left our table, my attention was focused elsewhere."

A stern expression invested Deven's nut-brown face. "I believe your orders include Silver LeMay, or someone very like her, Lieutenant."

"She presented herself as seductive and available, sir," I said dryly. "You know how susceptible I am when I'm on R&R."

"To be sure. I gather you feel pre-emptive action is not indicated."

"Not at this time, sir."

"And your reasoning?"

I made a face at the hologram. "LeMay was in the area for two days before Terreme was killed," I said, marshalling my points for myself as well as for Deven. "Had he been her target, she might have dispatched him at any time, unless it was important to her principals that he be killed in public on the beach. I'll concede that does remain a possibility, pending acquisition of more information. Assuming he was her target, she has no apparent reason to remain in the area. She also had a few opportunities to take me out, most particularly while my attention was focused on the Scritchy. Not only did she fail to do so, she pursued the seduction scene even afterwards. In fact . . . " I paused, as a notion flitted through and almost alighted.

"Your thought, Lieutenant," Deven prodded.

"I'm not that attractive, sir," I said slowly. "But I am safe."

For perhaps the third time in the seven years I had worked for Deven and the thirteen years I had known him, I had managed to startle him. "Look at it this way, sir," I continued quickly. "From her point of view, with me she can be who she is. We can talk shop, so to speak . . . editing a few things, of course."

Deven gave the explanation his seal of disapproval. "That sounds sentimental, Lieutenant."

"You and I both know what happens in bed, stays in bed, sir. But as I said, this is from her point of view. If sentimentality is involved, it's on her account, although I doubt that's the case." I ran my fingers through my hair, shaking out the loose ones and clearing my mind of cobwebs. Perhaps Deven was right: I might be overthinking this. Silver LeMay had not remained on Adenne for R&R or for me, but to complete whatever task she had contracted for. If it had something to do with me, it made sense for her to try to get me where she could keep an eye on me. Cobwebs cleared, I said, "Request, sir."

"Go ahead."

"Grenke's dossier, and any information we have on Frazier, first name not yet known. Whatever we can get on LeMay, including the nature of her assignment and who contracted her. Include Thone, too, please. Upload to Niobe."

"You'll have Grenke and Frazier presently," said Deven. "Thone may prove problematic, with so little to go on. As for LeMay, I'll initiate contact with the mortifice network, but they are notoriously reluctant to divulge information to outsiders." Here he paused for effect. "Ashler M. Tillvan, the Manager of AmResCor E&E, arrives at Port of Equatoria Spaceport on the schooner *Excel III* three evenings from now, your local time. There has not been nor will there be any public announcement. His dossier is being uploaded to Niobe as we speak. You are to remain in the background and prevent his assassination, taking whatever measures you deem necessary to do so."

Other hierarchs employ the vague phrasing to cover themselves in the event of failure by being able to blame their subordinates for exercising poor measure-taking judgment. Deven, on the other hand, actually means it. "Necessary," I said. "Yes, sir."

"It is preferred that you eliminate his assassin prior to the attempt, Lieutenant," Deven added. "You'll have Tillvan's projected itinerary in a few moments. Plan accordingly."

"Understood, sir."

"As for Silver LeMay," he went on, "I respect your judgment, Lieutenant, absent *specific* orders regarding her. However, her removal is an acceptable and even preferable action to take in order to ensure your ability to complete your assignment."

His hologram faded immediately after my acknowledgement, leaving me to ponder the problem of keeping someone alive. Usually the orders are quite simple: go there, kill that. It's the sort of task one person can easily carry out. Keeping someone alive, on the other hand, requires a team.

I heard the soft footsteps in the hallway just before the knock on my door. Frazier's voice came immediately, just as I took up the prescribed position. "Nyx, are you in there? Did you get back okay?"

I threw the door open. "You see me here."

Frazier looked startled, his eyes wide. It took him a moment to locate his voice. "I'm sorry," he said. "I had to talk with them. It's . . . it was . . . "

"Discourteous?" I supplied. "Inconsiderate?"

"I was going to say important, but it was that as well. May I . . . come in?"

I stepped aside, and shut the door behind him. "It's a bit late," I said. "What did you have in mind?"

Clearly he had not thought this through. "Well, I-I . . . maybe talk, and so forth."

"We've already talked," I told him, and shoved him backwards onto the bed. "Let's move on to the 'so forth.'"

004

Sunlight through open curtains awoke Frazier and me almost simultaneously. Muttering something about being late for duty, he slipped from the bed, wrapping himself in the top sheet. Apparently he deemed it necessary in daylight to conceal his two handfuls of tush while he skipped to the hygiene alcove. Moments later I heard water running, followed by the shower.

I swung my legs to the floor and sat up.

It was tempting to rummage through his clothing, which lay strewn where I had cast it, but I doubted I would find anything useful, and catching me during the search could work against future cooperation.

Still, I toed his handweapon--a Kellogg-Feuer, like Munro's--and finally flipped it over, noting the serial number.

Presently Frazier emerged, wearing the only bath towel, and eyed me expectantly. I got up and stepped to the alcove, a bit puzzled by his need for cover. Body consciousness after experiencing intimacies is inexplicable--to say nothing of inexcusable in an operative--but I had to concede that Frazier and I shared only a few elements of our respective professions. Well, modesty wasn't my problem, but as Deven would be sure to point out, one flaw hints at others.

To keep an eye on him while I was in the alcove, I tilted the mirror to just the right angle--if I could search his attire, presumably he could do the same to mine. The time it took me to clean my teeth allowed Frazier to dress, but he took no liberties.

"Don't forget your serving ware," I called, and watched him trudge across the room to the table. By the time I had finished, he was standing by the door, covered tray in hand.

Frazier would not look at me. Deven does not allow his operatives to be annoyed, but I was going to have to check the Table of Peeves to see if I had a hitherto-unknown allotment coming. "See you at the constabulary later today," I told him. He nodded, mumbled something, and left when I opened the door for him. When he reached the stairs, I pulled the door tight, the soft *snick* a starting point for the rest of the day.

Ablutions took a little time, chores associated with duties more so. The downloads from Deven--Tillvan's BI and itinerary, topographical holograms of the regions he planned to visit, the requested BI files on Frazier and Thone--gave me plenty of material to study, but little of it seemed germane to my mission. Manager Tillvan had earned two post-graduate degrees, in planetology and in spectrographic lithology, whatever that was, and had held the chair of Exploration & Exploitation Division, Amphictyony Resources Corporation, for eleven years. He still needed that one big coup that would advance him to upper management and, perhaps one day, the Chair of AmResCor. A widower, he had two daughters, Adelaide M. Day and Fluoranne Mantisse, neither residing with him. Blacklight Analysis--which also does not exist--regarded him as a corporate man who treated his family with benign neglect.

Danelik Thone had been born on Adenne and had lived here all his life. At the age of fifteen he quit school and went to work at the Spaceport, operating a cargo jack. His dossier revealed nothing untoward except fines for brawling and for public intoxication, the latter charge the result of having peed on a constable. Left to his own devices, he probably would retire after decades of loading and off-loading cargo.

Bryland Frazier, formerly an associate of the Putty Garson Syndicate on Tullis IV, had gone freelance three years ago, taking on a variety of odd jobs, some not as legitimate as others. The dossier summary described him as "intelligent muscle." Seen in that light, he would make an adequate constable. But what would Grenke want with him?

Frankl Grenke, also known as The Glacier, had a couple of decades of unsavory activities behind him, most of it "without attribution," meaning that he had not been detained, charged, and tried. He was still wanted for questioning here and there for non-capital offenses, none of which concerned Blacklight. Up until the past couple years he had usually operated in someone's employ. Lately, like Frazier, he had struck out on his own. Which meant that he was in Sayoun as more than a constable. It was by no means clear, however, that Grenke's presence on Adenne was related to my mission. As far as I could determine from his history, he had never killed anyone as a specific assignment, but only in conjunction with some other activity. Reportedly he was fond of beating people to death. It seemed unlikely, although not impossible, that he had targeted Ashler Tillvan.

A glance out the window told me that the pale red sun was halfway up the horizon, and I recalled that Silver LeMay had mentioned breakfast in the deli. Probably she had given up waiting, but I closed the dossier holograms, and finished dressing, set the telltales on my travelbag and incidentals, affixed the Maid Service note to the door, and clomped downstairs just in case.

LeMay was perched on a barstool at a corner table. To the casual observer she appeared innocuous, a comely young woman taking a few rays of mid-morning light along with a bagel and a frosted glass mug now only half-filled with ale. Today her attire motif was forest green, and she was dressed for the sun--shorts not quite as long as my cutoffs, and a jersey long and loose enough to conceal her weaponry. The pair of sturdy brown boots with deep treads that shod her feet suggested that she had a hike planned for later in the day. She had bound her hair with an emerald ribbon, and given her freshly-scrubbed look, I had to wonder why she did not already have company. Surely by now someone would have tried to sneak past her "I'm waiting for someone" and take a solid shot.

An experienced operative, on the other hand, would have noted that her position gave her a clear view through the window of the street outside and of the interior of the deli, and yet left her rear and right flank protected. Her right hand had unobstructed access to the Ecko 507 tucked under her belt, and I had to figure she had a knife of some kind in an ankle sheath. To me, she looked about as harmless as . . . well, a lioness.

LeMay smiled when she spotted me, and kept it flashed while I approached her table. With her in the strong right-hand position, I made a little adjustment under my jersey so that I could draw the Krupp Stern with my left hand, and sat down in the full sunlight directly in front of the window. The position left my back and right flank exposed, a necessary security compromise due to the potential threat confronting me.

With the adjustment, LeMay's smile faded, though her eyes-- battleship gray now--said that she understood. She made a little gesture. "You look like you need a drink and a lover."

I beckoned to the deli keep. "I'll take the drink," I said. "I've had the lover."

She slid her mug toward me, inviting me to take a gulp, and said, "You mean Frazier? You can do better than that."

The deli keep approached, a round, thick-fingered man with a receding hairline, and wearing a stained apron, the garment of his trade. Even his smile of greeting was beefy. I pointed to the remains of LeMay's order and asked for the same. After he lumbered off, she asked, "Did you reach your people?"

"My boss thinks I should remove you from the equation."

She popped the last bite of bagel into her mouth. "A prudent man, your boss."

"Didn't your principals advise the same with regard to me?"

"They had some advice," she conceded. "While I will listen to input, I carry out my contracts in my own way." Breakfast arrived, and while I addressed myself to it, she leaned back on the barstool. "If you don't mind telling me, what are your plans for today?"

I inspected the gap in the bagel that my first bite had left. Between the upper and lower halves lay slices of local meat and cheese, two slices of tomato, a broad and crunchy green leaf, a smear of orange condiment. As this was what LeMay had eaten, I said, "No onions?"

She looked at me, eyes shining with earnestness, and looked away. A little color crept into her cheeks. "Some people are put off by them," she said.

"I don't mind fighting fire with fire."

"I'll remember that at tomorrow's breakfast. Provided we're still alive," she added, as an afterthought.

"'We?'"

"I never count on tomorrows," said LeMay. "I just try to see the next one."

I took another bite of bagel and washed it down with half my ale. "Sure. Today I have to let an airfoil and do some recon."

"I already let one," said LeMay, the offer implicit.

"What color is it?"

She shot me a puzzled frown. "Red and gold," she answered. "Why?"

I gave her my best bland expression. "So I'll know it when I see it," I said easily. "Diana, my boss is going to have a stroke over this."

She leaned closer. "I won't tell," she said, hushed, "if you won't."

The promised airfoil was docked alongside the *Pestle*, and it appeared to be quite ordinary. LeMay powered up the fans after she performed the usual checks and initialization, and invited me to board up. I was beginning to relax just a little in her presence. Professionalism aside, you can stay tense and alert only for so long. I had to concede that her presence on Adenne might have nothing to do with me or my assignment.

I held onto a starboard taffrail as LeMay deftly swung the craft out over the main street and past the Constabulary. She was standing on the port side of the bridge, her left hand grasping the joystick, her right poised above the instrumentation console but within easy reach of her Ecko. I maintained a security watch over our flanks and rear as we passed between the rows of kiosks and diners. For just a moment I felt lonely. Here we were, two women who might have otherwise been on friendly terms, now traveling companions guardedly aware of one another and of our respective abilities. I had mentioned to Deven the possibility that LeMay saw me as at least a kindred spirit. Now, watching her at the controls, bare legs apart and braced, her long hair whipping in the breeze that curled around the plexishield, the hem of her jersey fluttering, I saw her lose for that lonely moment her identity as a mortifice and a potential adversary. Training told me that this loss simply could not be, nor could it be permitted. The moment said that an accommodation might be possible, but would require the active participation of both parties, a lowering of guards.

"Where are we going?" I asked her.

LeMay brought the airfoil to hover as we reached a small park just outside Sayoun. Here the glideways began, paths mowed and low overhanging branches cropped for the convenience of travelers. One led west to the ocean, another east to the Port of Equatoria Spaceport. "It's your recon," she pointed out.

I dug out the PHL and called up the coastal topography Deven had transmitted to me. The topogram spread behind us above the aft deck in a horizontal, realcolor map representing thirty kilometers on a side, with contours in three dimensions. Ocean occupied the left half of the map, the littoral escarpment of Equatoria the right. A strip of sand along the north-south axis separated the two.

I pointed to a notch in the coastline approximately halfway along the strip of sand. "That cove," I said, and disabled the topogram.

"North it is, then." She gave me a sideways glance as she threw the airfoil forward again, the crimson airspeed digits advancing toward thirty. "It's remote enough, and the current should take my body out to sea."

"If I wanted you dead, Silver, you'd already be dead."

She nodded. "I keep telling myself that. I imagine you say much the same thing with regard to me. And here on Adenne it's Diana. I'm only Silver in bed."

"I'll remember that."

"I hope you have a chance to."

"Stop."

"Me, or the airfoil?"

"Hover."

She grinned. "Definitely the airfoil," she said, and eased the airspeed back down before turning to face me on the bridge. "Now what?" she asked brightly.

LeMay didn't even flinch when I tugged the Krupp Stern from under my jersey. Briefly I looked at it, then slipped it back. "I can't think of anything to do with this that wouldn't be melodramatic," I said slowly. The nebula in her eyes had faded now, and I wondered what she saw in mine. "If I chucked it aft, and my knife, and invited you to do the same, we'd still have our physical skills. Silver . . . Diana, we can't declare peace, or even a truce. It wouldn't mean anything, to either of us."

"Frustrating, isn't it?"

"I'm under orders to eschew frustration."

"What a pity. I know a great way to relieve it."

"North," I told her. "Please."

LeMay looked at me for so long a time that I wondered whether she had heard me. Her expression told me nothing. The luster in her eyes came not from some inner fire, but from the reflection of sunlight. Presently her shoulders slumped, ever so slightly, in resignation. Her left hand probed a utility bin, and came out with a pair of cammie bush hats, one of which she passed to me. As I fitted it to my head, I realized that I had lowered my guard considerably, and for a brief and apprehensive second my right hand darted of its own accord toward the Stern under my jersey. LeMay merely watched me, a crooked smile on her face, a bit of mirth playing in her eyes. I decided to move on to the next moment, there being nothing I might say to improve the present one.

"So?" I said, struggling with the turned-down brim.

"I'd love to see you in that," she said softly.

"I *am* in it."

"That's not what I meant . . . never mind. Personal kink." LeMay swung the airfoil inland, and raised the groundhug application to two meters of clearance to accommodate irregularities in the terrain. "Shall we take the scenic route?" she asked.

"I'd rather not dawdle," I told her, and she pushed the joystick forward.

Two minutes later we passed the last of the mixed forest that encircled Sayoun, and burst out onto a wind-swept, sand-covered plains on which sparse tufts of blue-green grass seemed to thrive. Here and there, gnarled and misshapen trees stubbornly eked out a meager existence. To the northeast rose rocky foothills, and granite boulders gleamed under the mid-day light from the pale red dwarf that Adenne circled. The coastline soon began to curve inwards, and already I could smell the brine and a bit of decomposition. The land was still elevated, and concealed the shoreline from us, but in the distance to the west I could see the ocean, a glistening blue expanse to the horizon. I could even hear the waves, although that might have been my imagination, for we were still a good kilometer from shore.

"I could retire around here," allowed LeMay.

"You and me both."

After a beat of perhaps two seconds, both of us burst into laughter. LeMay recovered first, and managed a strangled, "Or not. That's the problem with our professions, Nyx. We're not expected to outlive them."

"You did mention the tomorrows," I said.

On the plains, the glideway faded into oblivion. LeMay banked the airfoil about twenty degrees to the west, taking us shoreward. Gusts from the ocean began to buffet the airfoil. I threw a glance aft. Over a kilometer behind us rose a wake of sand as the airfoil that presumably was trailing us reached the plains. I said, "Diana."

"I see it," she acknowledged. "I was wondering whether you would tell me." Again she fumbled in the utility bin, and this time withdrew a pair of binox, which she passed to me.

The unsteadiness of our airfoil made focusing difficult. There appeared to be one person in the craft behind us, attired in white and blue. I could make out short brown hair, pale skin, and a slight build, but no features and no gender.

"I don't think I know him," I said. "Want me to take the controls so you can have a look?"

LeMay shook her head. "He's maintaining his distance. We'll get a better look after we reach the cove in about four more minutes. And Nyx . . . "

"When the tail is that obvious, be alert for one that's hidden," I said.

"I'm not accustomed to working with another pro."

"We should break off and head northeast, toward those foothills," I said, pointing. "There's no cover here, especially if he has that rifle."

"Rifle? Ah, yes, the shooting on the beach, and later at the Constabulary." She gave me a sidelong look, though she did not alter course. "And you were present on both occasions."

Ahead of us stood several wind-sculpted trees, and LeMay negotiated our way through them with fine insouciance while I leaned, unnecessarily, with the turns. "I'm not sure what you mean by that," I said. "He may have that rifle, but you're the only person here on Adenne who would know for certain that it would be a really good idea to kill me."

Moments later LeMay brought the airfoil to hover, and said, "Look down there, Nyx."

We had reached the remains of an ancient escarpment. Below us opened a cove, as if some marine giant had taken a bite out of the coastline. The escarpment along the north margin consisted of broken granite marked with long, slanting black lines that were swallowed up by the sand at the back of the cove. Our current viewing angle did not permit a sight of the south margin, but I supposed it to be similar. Several trees grew out of the base of the margins, and offered a bit of shade to visitors. Off to our right, part of the escarpment had given way, and we might descend at that point in the airfoil to the beach if we wished, or perhaps climb down on foot.

"Idyllic," I said, with a glance behind us. The trailing airfoil had paused, still a kilometer away. At that range a rifle shot would have been almost but not quite impossible, now that we were hovering. I continued to look around for anything I might have missed, but the only concealment lay on the beach beyond the escarpment. Deven had said that Tillvan and AmResCor were interested in this area, but I saw nothing that screamed for exploitation.

On that beach, the tide was out, and you could see where the waves had worn smooth the base of the north escarpment. Narrow horizontal bands of color indicated the higher and average splash points of the waves. The sand itself was a yellowish tan, not that pale white you see on long, flat beaches. The waves peaked and seemed to collapse upon themselves as they rolled up the sand, and deposited a blanket of white froth that quickly dissipated before the next wave arrived.

I passed LeMay the binox. "I used to own a couple of seascape prints," she said, dialing the focus. "Both by Richards, twenty-first century artist. Do you know her work?"

"I've heard the name," I said. "Used to?"

"At one time I thought I might set up a private gallery, for my own enjoyment and, perhaps, for a guest to appreciate. Ah, but whom to invite?" She reached a setting she liked. "Hello! That looks like Agate."

"Who is?" I prodded.

"She's a true believer from Ecotect," said LeMay, wrinkling her nose in mild disapproval. "Saving the universe, one environmental disaster at a time, she and her companion Kitch . . . although Agate seems to have come alone. Usually you see both girls together."

I took the binox for a better look. Even with the airfoil steady, Agate's features remained blurred. Still, she looked familiar, and I struggled to place her.

"Full names?"

"Agate and Kitch are all I know."

"And what makes them Ecotect?"

LeMay took the binox back and placed them in the bin. "That white pullover Agate is wearing has a likeness of this very cove, and a caption exhorting people to save our coastline.. Also, she and Kitch have attended the last two beach bonfire rallies, although only a few people showed up."

"Rallies you observed?" LeMay's thin lips pursed, and I added, "Diana, if you know something, tell me. Or are you under contract?"

"Not in the way you mean," she said. "I attended one rally, not to see who was there, but to get a feel for the event. They seem peaceful, if quite vocal." She gave me a cautious look. "Are we reciprocating on information, then?" At my shrug, she continued, "You said this was a recon. What's so special about this cove?"

"I don't know," I answered truthfully. "The background info I received said that Terreme was interested in it and in this general area." I stopped myself before I mentioned Tillvan's arrival, but LeMay was intuitive.

"You wouldn't have come out here to see this," said LeMay, with a little shake of her head, then gazed at me, searching my face for confirmation. "Unless AmResCor is sending a replacement for Terreme. He, too, will be interested in this area."

Suddenly the distant airfoil powered up and made for the rocky foothills half a kilometer northeast of our position. Without hesitation Silver LeMay sent us hurtling after her. Given the angle of pursuit, and the roughly equal capabilities of our respective crafts, we had no chance of overtaking her, but we might learn where she was headed. Alert to the possibility that Agate's headlong flight was meant to distract us from danger to our rear, I kept a watchful eye out, and left the navigation to LeMay.

Presently I heard a little sound of satisfaction. "She's slowing, hovering . . . and stopped," said LeMay. "Nyx, I believe our girl wants to talk."

"Or trap us," I said.

"Yes, of course," agreed LeMay. "There is that to consider."

Avoiding boulders and outcrops, she took us up onto a saddle between two foothills, where Agate, having already descended from her craft, awaited us. A pair of scraggly trees stood guard at the lowest point of the saddle, sentries of vegetation in an otherwise hostile environment, as nothing else save lichens and a few wildflowers had gained a foothold here. LeMay brought our airfoil to hover, and downed her onto a patch of sand, slowing the fans until they no longer threw up clouds of grit.

Agate was wearing, of all things, a pair of bib dungarees and a white pullover, and beach sandals, and looked even younger than my estimate of seventeen. Her lanky frame could have tolerated another couple of kilograms, and she had looked agile enough when she climbed out of the airfoil. She waited patiently for us to approach, hands at her sides and clearly empty. She could not know precisely who and what we were, of course, but she eyed us warily, as if we were somehow on official business. When we reached her, she turned around, facing away from the ocean, to keep the late morning sun off her pale face. Already her snub nose had begun to redden.

Her voice came low, but determined. "You won't stop us," she said. "No matter how many of us you kill, we will not allow Amphictyony Resources Corporation to exploit this coastline."

"She's Diana," I said, "and I'm Nyx. What makes you think we care what you or AmResCor do?"

Agate turned deep blue eyes to me, and blinked. "But you were there when that man was killed. That's your excuse to start killing us."

Her logic was interesting, if faulty. I said, "If that were true, then you've taken a huge risk by following us, by inviting us here."

The girl licked her dry lips. "I wanted to let you know," she said bravely.

"We're both on R&R," LeMay informed her.

Agate just looked at her. "I saw you the other night, watching us."

LeMay shrugged. "I was on the beach, and so were you. We'd still like to know why you even think we're interested in you."

Agate's eyes darkened while she pondered her response. Suddenly I heard an ugly sound, like an axe being swung into a large roast, and in that same moment the girl plunged forward, her shoulder slamming into me, and spilling her sideways. She fell with her head back, and landed face down on the sand and gravel, sliding perhaps half a meter, without having lifted her hands to break her fall. She lay completely soft and flattened, and I heard the report from somewhere seaward of us. LeMay lunged for the airfoil, powering it up while I scrambled aboard and then ducked down. Beside me squatted LeMay, maneuvering the airfoil as best she could, unable to see over the console. Something struck a solid blow against the stern, and plastic shattered. LeMay's shoulders stiffened in anticipation as she shot to her feet for a quick look ahead, then dropped to her knees again, easing the joystick to starboard. We banked, grazed one of the guardian trees, and dropped behind the hillock.

Stern in hand, I leaped from the airfoil and started back up the slope toward a cluster of granite boulders on the crest that might offer sufficient cover. I hadn't gotten halfway when LeMay tackled me and drove me into the gravel. I rolled over, slammed a knee into her cheek that seemed to startle her and knock her from me. Another roll brought me on top of her, straddling her, left hand on her weapon shoulder, the Stern aimed at the bridge of her nose.

"*What?*" was all I could manage

Somewhat to my surprise LeMay relented, and flashed a grin. "This is hardly the time," she said, and gave my pelvis a little nudge with hers. Her outstretched right hand was curled around the butt of her Ecko. but she made no effort to bring it to bear. "She's dead, Nyx," she added, sobering. "There's no need to check."

"I *know*," I said, still annoyed, and she gave me an apologetic nod. I also knew what I would find if I examined the body: a hole between her shoulder blades, the massive bullet exploding her spinal fluid, blowing her brain dark in a nanosecond. She'd had no chance. But why kill her?

Under me, LeMay shifted. "Better let me up. We need to go find out what he's doing."

We scrabbled up to the boulders, and crouched well below the tops of them. Once more, LeMay's eyes were battleship gray, and unreadable. "I'm going to have a look," she announced.

"Be careful," I said--unnecessarily. Like her, I was unaccustomed to working with another pro.

Her face brightened momentarily. "Why, yes. I will."

On impulse I rose with her. If the shooter was offered two targets, it might give him a better chance to miss both of them. We ducked back

47

after half a second. Presently I heard a ricochet scream like a banshee, again followed by a report. Evidently he had removed the sound suppressor.

"Total amateur," muttered LeMay.

During that brief glimpse I had seen an airfoil bearing in our direction. Someone was standing on the bridge, rifle braced against his shoulder. Another bullet struck the boulder that covered me, solidly this time. I chanced a peek around the side of it this time, and dodged back.

As ludicrous as it was to sacrifice his overwhelmingly superior advantage in weapons range, the shooter was also trying to aim a scoped weapon at a target he was approaching at high speed, while standing on an airfoil in an uneven breeze. It was a wonder he could even hit the boulders. If he spotted us at all through the scope, it would be as shadows, chimera. I guessed it had not occurred to him that we might be armed.

"About 200 meters now," I said, and hefted the Stern. "About ten seconds away. My range is about twenty-five. What's the Ecko, around thirty?"

LeMay grunted. Another round raised a shower of gravel that arced over the boulders and tumbled down the back slope. She rose, took a look, ducked back.

"Less than a hundred now," she said. "We go after the next shot. Smoke one quickly if you have it."

The next bullet missed everything, and we heard the hiss as it passed overhead. LeMay and I rose as one, firing our initial beams without aiming, but roughly at the spot where we figured the airfoil to be. Painted desert camouflage, it had drawn within twenty-five meters and slowed, climbing the front slope of the hillock. He was now trying to aim and fire with one hand while controlling the craft with the other. Our blue beams caromed off the bow.

"I prefer to fire up a cherry cheroot when I'm relaxed," I replied, shouting, my voice powered by adrenalin, as I fired again and missed.

LeMay's next beam caught the man flush on the hip, and he spun around, dropping the rifle. "I take a briar pipe stuffed with maple blend, myself," she countered, just as loudly.

The airfoil yawed to starboard. I had a clear shot at the shooter's torso, and I took it. "I have a smooth single malt that should go with that," I yelled.

Her beam followed mine home, and the man fell aft onto the deck, vanishing from view. "Is that an invitation?"

The airfoil was bearing down sideways on our position now, but I turned to look at her. "Maybe."

"That's an improvement over 'no.'" She flashed a wicked grin. "Nyx?"

"What?"

"Run!"

We were halfway down the slope, stumbling, when the craft struck the boulders. The impact was massive. Plastic shattered, and metal crumpled, and fragments made a rainbow over the crest. The man sprawled across the top boulder, and the stern scoured him off it, gouging his body. An irregular sheet of plastic wobbled toward us. LeMay shoved me aside and blocked the fragment with her left arm, and swore. Midway between her wrist and elbow, a pink mark quickly formed, soon to be a bruise.

After the hail of shards ceased, I climbed back up to examine the body. Behind me, gravel yielded as LeMay followed. It occurred to me that I had let my guard down badly. That sort of development could not be omitted from my after-action report, and Deven was going to empty half his thesaurus of harsh words on it. LeMay caught me up just as I reached the body.

The shooter was attired simply, in shirt, slacks, and shoes, and looked somewhat familiar. His face was a mess, and although he appeared to be unconscious, his chest heaved with the autonomic effort of trying to draw air through a crushed larynx. Blood seeped through gashes and gouges too numerous to count, and I reckoned many if not most of his bones had been broken. LeMay knelt beside him and began rummaging through his pockets, coming up with a thin white facecloth, several local coins, a box of .444 cartridges, and two or three globs of lint.

"He's still alive, barely," she said.

"I can fix that," I told her, and fired a blue beam into his face.

LeMay stood up. "I don't think he followed us here," she said, as I collected his rifle, and we headed back to her airfoil. "I think he was lurking down in that cove." She paused, and looked at me. "Nyx, I have the feeling I've seen him before, but I can't quite place him."

"Same here. Maybe it'll come to you during that pipe."

She flashed a grin. "I was hoping you'd do that." Then: "What do you want to do about the bodies?"

"Let's keep our ears to the ground and see who complains," I suggested, as we climbed back aboard the airfoil.

"Someone should tell Kitch about her . . . friend."

I scowled at her. "Sentimental?"

"Wash your mouth out. No, but as you're looking for reactions, it might be interesting to see hers."

"And if this Kitch knew that Agate was tailing us to the cove, it could complicate my mission," I pointed out. "I don't want some lovelorn adolescent coming after me . . . us, Diana."

"Oh, I like that recovery." Her smile faded. "In any case, when Agate doesn't return, Kitch will search for her."

"Can you get word to her quietly, maybe? Let her know the killer was an unidentified male?"

LeMay completed the last of the initialization process and brought the airfoil to hover. "It'll buy some time, at any rate. As this is your idea, if she has any questions, I'll just send her to you. Now: where to?"

"The constabulary," I told her. She shot me a puzzled glance, and I explained, "I promised Grenke I would stop by today, in case they had more questions. After that, I'll want to report in."

While LeMay swung the airfoil around the hillock and aimed it in the general direction of Sayoun, I hefted the rifle. The barrel had bent, and the scope had shattered, leaving only the attachments. The overall condition of the weapon was a damned shame. A Marlin 1895, it had been a fine piece before the impact with the boulders. I got the lever to work and ejected but one round. As the Marlin had a six-round tube, and I had counted five shots, including the one that killed Agate, he had not carried a round in the pipe before coming after us, another mark of the amateur.

I stowed the rifle under one of the aft benches. "Keep that here for me, please," I told her. "I may have use for it later."

"It looks like it came from a museum, or a collection," allowed LeMay.

I recalled that she had considerable expertise with firearms. "It might have, at that," I said noncommittally.

"No more recon today?"

"I don't know yet. Is there a speed governor on this thing?"

LeMay increased the fan pitch and rate, and the acceleration swiftly incremented the crimson digits that indicated the groundspeed. The wind around the plexishield made conversation difficult, but I realized I did not have a lot to say at the moment. Too much had transpired in too short a time, and it needed mulling and reporting. As I've indicated, operatives do not go running to Deven whenever they are shot at, but it now appeared certain that someone wanted me out of the way, and I didn't think it was Ecotect. And the only other person I knew of on Adenne who might benefit from my death was standing beside me on the bridge of the airfoil.

005

Grenke was not in the constabulary when I arrived, after seeing LeMay off, presumably back to her room in the *Pestle*. At his desk sat a sullen young man in a green and brown uniform that had already seen some duty today. Even his harness looked dull. He spoke in a tone that matched his uniform.

"Name and business?"

"Nyx, and none of yours," I told him. "I'm here to see the constable. Is he expected back soon?"

He shook his head, but I had no idea how long a wait that indicated. He started to pursue the matter of my identification when I spotted an airfoil docking outside. Like the one the late Associate Constable Munro had piloted, this one was also powder blue. I caught a glimpse of a large shape descending, and in the next moment Constable Grenke shoved the front door open and entered. A jerk of his thumb punctuated his order of "Outside, Kellar. Check the parks for light fingers."

The young man got up and left, and Grenke sat down audibly. He looked displeased. Since the last time I had seen him, his left eye had acquired a tic. He placed his thick hands flat on the desk top and leaned forward, gazing up at me the way a shrike eyes a minnow. "Your personnel folder at Ways & Means speaks very highly of you," he said.

"I try to stay out of trouble."

"But my source at Ways & Means has never heard of you," Grenke went on, as if I had not spoken. "In fact, nobody there has."

"My home is my office," I told him, which was true, as far as it went.

Again he ignored me. "Covers like that are usually set up by one of the corporate security divisions." He paused briefly, eyes narrowed. "I don't suppose you'll tell me why you are here."

"I came here for a few days of R&R, Constable," I answered.

"You'd say that in any event."

I shrugged. Grenke was right, of course. But my cover with Ways & Means is standard default when I'm not on assignment, when that cover is unlikely to be checked further than my credentials. Had I needed a deeper cover while on furlough, Deven would have devised one. On the other hand, an operative's cover is not generally worth risking life and limb to preserve. If Grenke truly wanted to know my identity, I have a second default at Amphictyony Security, who would tell him to back the hell off. I could not, of course, reveal my association with Blacklight, because we do not exist.

For a moment it was tempting to distract him by letting him know that I was aware of his unsavory background, but I quickly discarded that idea. He might display all the trappings of a village constable, but he undoubtedly had something else going for him here on Adenne, and might conclude that my awareness was a liability. Already I was tired of strangers shooting at me while I was on furlough. I did not need anyone else gunning for me.

I decided to phrase my questions carefully, to avoid giving Grenke any notion that I knew he was more than a constable. "Have you identified the weapon that killed Terreme on the beach?"

Grenke gave me a silent count of five before answering. A welt appeared across his forehead as muscles bunched, and his dark eyebrows merged like rutting caterpillars. "Large caliber, high-powered bullet," he said at last, with some reluctance. "It passed completely through him. I'm not going to waste time sending an associate to the beach with a metal detector."

"Have you turned up anyone on Adenne with a collection of old weapons?"

Again there was a pause. "No one here in Sayoun," he replied, as the caterpillars separated. "I've made inquiries with the other communities on Adenne, so far without positive response."

"Of course, the rifle could have been imported from almost anywhere."

"Of course. And it's an easier weapon for Ecotect to acquire."

That had not occurred to me. "Why do you suppose that?"

His pauses began to annoy me, but Deven cautions us against throttling unless it is indicated by mission requirements. Finally Grenke said, "They're less expensive to purchase in the underground markets, for one thing. For another, private collections and museums generally have lower levels of security than military and security installations." Grenke tilted his chair back. His scowl said that he was done with explanations. "How many more days of R&R do you have here?"

"Five or six," I said. "It's kind of open-ended."

"Two people have been shot dead while you were around," he reminded me, staying in constable mode. Either he had not yet been informed of the killings near the cove, or he was testing whether I knew. "Shortening your vacation might save lives."

"I shall bear that in mind, Constable. Is there anything else?"

"Your early departure is more than a suggestion, *M'selle* Nyx. Sayoun may not be the most comfortable place for you."

"I shall bear that in mind as well."

Rather to my surprise, Silver LeMay was waiting for me when I emerged from the Constabulary. In the struggle to keep my hand from diving for the Stern, I probably looked as if I were fidgeting. Evidently the expression on my face did not encourage conversation, so she powered up the airfoil and took us back to the *Pestle* in silence. Before disembarking, I tried to return the bush hat to her, but she waved it off.

"I'll be in the deli," she told me, rather stiffly, and I nodded.

The Maid Service note was gone from my door. I had left no telltales on the door or touchpad, there being no point to them. An examination of the door and jamb revealed nothing of concern. I entered in the prescribed manner, and came up with the Stern aimed at the room in general. Finally, after searching the room and scanning with the PHL for surreptitious devices, I raised Deven.

"Describe the weapon," he said, his hologram standing in the center of the room, after I had reconstructed the events of the day.

I gave him the nomenclature and serial number, and added, "It takes what's listed as a .444 cartridge, sir, but in actual measurement it's a .429. That's the old style of measurement. Think of it as a 10.9 mike-mike, sir. Plastic tipped, and with a relatively flat trajectory, ideal for long range."

"The information is being transferred to the archivist even as we speak," he said. "Describe the shooter."

I did so, and added Agate's description as well. It was not much to go on. "Grenke strongly suggested that I cut short my furlough, sir," I told him.

Deven looked at me sharply. "Do you feel rested already, Lieutenant?"

"Weak as a kitten, sir."

"As to the matter of Silver LeMay," he went on. "You mentioned that her airfoil was the same color as the one you saw leaving the beach area yesterday."

"But the man who shot at us was in a cammie airfoil, sir."

"That does not eliminate LeMay as a suspect in Terreme's killing, Lieutenant. In any case, we've heard back from the mortifice network." The corners of his mouth turned down maybe a millimeter, a sure sign of his concern. "We were not informed of the specific nature of the contract, but LeMay was hired by Ecotect."

"Where did they get the money?"

"Ecotect has a number of large donors," Deven reminded me. "Many are dilettantes, eager for association with what appears to be a good cause. I daresay once they learn their donations have purchased the services of a professional assassin, they may wish to dissociate themselves." He paused, and gave me a hard look. "Find Silver LeMay and make the nock," he ordered, employing the current euphemism.

"Yes, sir. Question, sir."

"Go ahead."

"How do we know that Ecotect is behind the killing of Manager Terreme?"

"In point of fact, we do not," he conceded. "But that is irrelevant to your orders. Those who have tasked us feel that her removal will serve to ensure the safety of Manager Tillvan. We shall comply."

"Sir---"

"Make the nock, Lieutenant. Make contact with me after you have done so."

"Yes, sir."

After Deven's hologram faded, I went to the window and gazed out on the street. LeMay's airfoil remained where she had docked it, basking now in the afternoon sunlight, so presumably she was still in the deli, waiting for me. Deven prefers that, whenever possible, we avoid drawing attention to ourselves, and the deli was too public a place for me to carry out my orders. My heart weighed like a clenched fist. For a few brief and poignant moments Silver LeMay had forced an awareness onto me of the utter loneliness of our professions, and had suggested that it was possible to engage in a relationship in which mutual trust was not a prerequisite. Training had not been specific on the issue of relationships, it being generally assumed that these were matters of artifice, or at best of convenience. We all have itches that need scratching. Frazier had been a *loofah* body buff, useful insofar as he went. Silver LeMay promised to be a long-handled bath brush, able to reach areas otherwise difficult to scour. That promise said we might indulge, if we could keep from killing each other.

Deven's orders had put an end to that potential. That the orders satisfied a mission requirement that might not have to be met was scant consolation. Worse for me, and for the stone that my heart had become, they offered no wiggle room. Meanwhile, Ashler Tillvan was not due to arrive for another two full days. I thought about that, and about the wording of my orders. I had been told to find Silver LeMay. Very well: perhaps she was on the beach, working on her tan. I decided to go look.

Getting out of *The Silver Pestle* unseen posed no great problem, provided the fire escape did not sound an alarm when opened. After securing my room I crept down the hallway away from LeMay's room. Nothing about the door suggested an alarm; nevertheless, I cringed as I pushed on the door. It opened almost soundlessly, and gave onto a landing from which black steps of wrought iron descended to a flower garden and a small cluster of low junipers. Few people were about, and those mostly retirees out for a stroll. To avoid LeMay spotting me through the deli window, I took the back way around the inn and came out beside a refreshment kiosk.

So far during this R&R I had taken public transportation to the beach, and relied on LeMay to get me to the inlet. It was time to promote my own transportation and the independence of movement and action that accompanied it. At the kiosk I purchased a miniature bottle of peppermint schnapps and inquired as to where I might let an airfoil, and received directions. The schnapps downed in one bracing gulp, I followed the boardwalk along the main glideway east until I came to the recommended lot, identified by a sign above the office door that read Emmix Transport. The office itself was little more than a prefab storage conex that someone had painted a hideous orange. Of far more interest were the vehicles docked on the lot. All were airfoils, and all were red and gold.

A moment of weakness tugged at me. I entertained a vision of raising Deven to point out that Terreme's killer could not be identified by the color of the airfoil involved, that the order against Silver LeMay might be premature. But that illusory moment passed, training having re-imposed focus, as it was supposed to do. While Deven will listen to an operative in the field, once he barks, we bite. I permitted myself one thought-free moment during which I put my hand over my heart to settle it down, then entered the lot and made for the Emmix office.

At the open doorway I peered around the jamb until I spotted the attendant seated on a stool behind a counter, focused on a hologram on a shelf at lap-level, though all I could see of it was the glow. From where I stood, he was wearing at least a faded blue work shirt sealed down the front. When he glanced up and noticed me, he issued a terse, "Off," and the glow from the hologram vanished. His face was flushed, his medium long black hair a bit tousled. His expression declared that he knew that I knew the nature of the entertainment in which he had been absorbed, and that he dared me to remark upon it. Finally he cleared his throat, and asked whether he might be of assistance.

I looked around. The storage conex, as I thought of it, was sparsely furnished: the counter, two stools, an administrative computer for registrations, and a vending machine against the back wall that dispensed various beverages, some of them alcoholic, and snacks--but no security or surveillance devices. On the wall next to the vending machine hung a poster that promoted a romantic fantasy entertainment 'gram, its colors faded by age and by the afternoon sunlight that now beamed in through the only window. The air smelled like a laundry bin of dirty towels outside the shower in a gym.

I approached the counter just close enough to see over it and determine that he had no weapons in his hands or on the shelf. "I'd like to let an airfoil for a couple days," I told the attendant. "Three at most, I should think."

He did not allow his eyes to meet mine. "When do you want it?"

"Now, if possible."

"I have to charge you for a full day for today, you understand. It's policy."

I doubted that, but withheld comment in the hope of eliciting information later. I presented my Ways & Means credentials and a fundscard so that he could complete the registration template and deduct the let fee in advance, along with incidentals such as damage and injury. While he processed my data, I said, "I don't suppose you would have a list of names of people who have let airfoils over the past two days or so."

He paused, and peered up at me through half-lidded, pale blue eyes. "I might," he allowed.

I drew a clip of folded currency from my pocket and peeled a purple and yellow AV100 note from it. Probably the money represented only a couple hours work for him, but I reckoned it was enough. "Might you indeed?" I said, and laid the note on the counter top.

The attendant's hand swept it up immediately. He issued a brief instruction to the admincomp and presently I heard a low hum as the information printed out. Evidently he did not want to risk an upload that might be traced. Meanwhile he passed me the palmer for approval of the lease agreement. The green plastic casing felt clammy from handling, and fingerprints smeared the tiny monitor. The data in the monitor was legible enough, and indicated the airfoil model number, my name and fundscard number, the terms and conditions of the lease, and the total of the fees to be deducted from my account. I keyed for a receipt to be transmitted to Niobe, the 'skipcomp aboard my *Kuremsha*, and ticked approval with a fingertip before returning the palmer to him. That transaction completed, he then handed me a half-sheet of paper bearing three names, none of them known to me. Evidently this was the slow season for airfoil leases.

"That's all?" I asked. "Just these three?"

"You wanted people," he said defensively. "Not tours or local renewals."

"Petar Logrin and Edam Windle," I said, reading the list, "and McKittrick Day. Who are they?"

The attendant just looked at me.

I peeled another AV100 note free and laid it on the counter top. When he tried to collect it I snatched his wrist, twisting it to apply pressure to the ulnar nerve. He frowned at first, but then alarm widened his eyes as he realized it hurt worse to try to pull away. "Talk first," I snarled. "Who are they?"

He licked his lips. "Windle, he's a tourist. He's looking to retire here, maybe."

"Maybe?"

"That's what he said. Logrin is new, but local. Works here. I don't know McKitt---"

"Works where?"

The pain in his eyes reflected the additional pressure on his wrist. "I don't know," he cried. "I don't! That's the truth! I've seen him around a couple times. One of the inns, maybe, or out at the Spaceport, they're always hiring."

"Description?"

He blinked, thinking. "I didn't get that good a look, I-I . . . shorter than you. Medium build. Dark hair."

"What about this Windle? And where can I find him?"

He shook his head. "He's a tourist. Where do tourists go? He's small, smaller than me, and overweight. Some gray hair, I remember that. Light eyes, I think."

"Where's he staying?"

"He didn't--didn't say." He grimaced in pain. "Stop. Just--please stop."

I held on. "And Day?"

"I don't know. I *don't*." His words came quickly now, his voice pitched higher. "I wasn't here for that registration. It was Callan, he'll know. He works tomorrow, he can tell you."

"Thank you." I released his wrist and the AV100. "Now, where's my transportation?"

He pointed, and instinctively I knocked his arm away. "It's--number seventeen, outside and--and turn right," he told me, his eyes accusing me while he rubbed his elbow. "The second airfoil on your right. The number is stenciled on the stern."

I stepped outside cautiously, looking for Silver LeMay. She was nowhere in sight, which meant nothing, but at least she was not strolling up to me, intent on a friendly encounter. I found the airfoil, climbed aboard, and initiated the power sequences. For a moment I wondered whether the attendant, in a bit of passive resistance, might have assigned me a craft with defects, but the console indicators read within normal parameters. I felt under the console until I located the fuse box, and disabled the Programmed Destination Feature--because the same system that tells you where you are, tells *them* where you are. All that remained was for me to pick a direction.

I chose east, taking the glideway that bisected Sayoun, intending to skirt north around the settlement and then west, back to the coastline. As I reached the limits of Sayoun, I changed my mind, altered course, and bore for the Port of Equatoria Spaceport. It lay some ten kilometers due east, where the terrain was naturally level. From the topogram I imagined the region might have once been an inland sea, now a salt flat. In a straightaway now, I pushed the airfoil to 150, though I was in no particular hurry, and checked periodically for tails, finding none. Here the glideway was little more than a strip across the terrain, outlined by stones that had been daubed with fluorescent paint to facilitate travel by night. By the time I had closed to within five kilometers, the Spaceport had come into focus as a low skyline of warehouses interspersed with the trappings of interstellar travel: stay-the-nights, shops, a terminal, a maintenance derrick. With Sayoun little more than a primitive and low-tech town, the Port of Equatoria Spaceport seemed a bit ostentatious. A smaller facility would have been much more practical, to say nothing of less expensive. Still, it did service not only Sayoun, but the other settlements on the continent, including the other resort towns along the west coast. I wondered whether an increase in tourism was in the offing.

At one kilometer out I swung the airfoil south, off the glideway, bypassing the Spaceport in favor of checking out its surrounding terrain to compare it to that on the topogram. Circling at approximately 500 meters from the Spaceport, I looked for any features that might be utilized as cover for sniper fire. In a salt flat, I hardly expected to find any, though there might be a shallow wash that would suffice. But a wash or even a gully would not have provided concealment for the transportation the sniper required to get away afterwards. Given the lack of features in this terrain, I could not envision a sniper attack on Tillvan when he arrived at the Spaceport.

After returning to the glideway, I brought the airfoil to hover, contemplating the possibilities. A sniper attack on the incoming AmResCor representative had to be regarded as a suicide mission. This would render escape transportation unnecessary. Firing was also problematic. At 500 meters, it would take a bullet just over a second to reach its target. A man walking at three kilometers an hour would move just under a meter in the time the bullet took to arrive. The shot could be made if the target remained stationary. At that distance, firing at a moving target--or a target about to move--was iffy. Worse, if the first bullet missed and alerted the target, he could cover perhaps nine meters in a second while fleeing, making a follow-up kill shot virtually impossible. The terrain between the salt flat and Sayoun was a little more rugged, and there were a few trees that might provide cover and gullies concealment, but here the sniper would perforce be firing at a moving target--far from a certain kill.

At this point I had to pause and rethink. I was assuming the weapon involved would be a high-powered rifle similar to the Marlin, with a long range, red-dot scope. But an ergorifle was also a possibility. The maximum effective range of the Kreisler-Post, the top-of-the-line model, was 250 meters, give or take a meter or two. Obviously, it required the sniper to post himself or herself closer to the target, but its advantage over the rifle was the instantaneity of killing fire. The blue beams from energy weapons travel at the speed of light. Under that circumstance, the red dot you see in the scope sight picture is what you get, whether the target is moving or stationary. With an ergorifle, then, it was still a suicide mission at the Spaceport, but much less so en route to Sayoun, where the terrain allowed the sniper to hide an escape vehicle.

All this was conjecture, of course, based on the instances that had already occurred. Someone had used a rifle on the beach and at the constabulary. Someone--perhaps the same person--had used a rifle at the cove. Suddenly I had a eureka moment, although I was in the dark as to where it led: why use a rifle at all? The only possible answer I could see was that Tillvan was not going to be killed by a sniper attack, but by one of any number of other means. A Scritchy in his door. Pulled under while swimming. Poisoned in a tavern. Unfortunately, to investigate those alternatives, I needed more information regarding Tillvan's itinerary, and Deven was my source for it. And if I raised him, the first question out of his mouth would be an inquiry into the status of one Silver LeMay.

The pale red sun was just above the horizon now. I'd left the day too late to go to the beach for the ruse of searching for LeMay. I had no idea where she was right now. As far as I could tell, I was alone on the glideway. We're not supposed to feel hunger or depression, but my stomach was muttering and my heart still weighed like a stone. I could not assuage either of those by remaining where I was.

006

On the return to Sayoun I encountered a public conveyance headed for the Spaceport. It looked like the one I had ridden in to Sayoun after I arrived Two days ago. This one was empty, save for the operator, and presumably was bound to pick up more tourists. The glideway was wide enough to accommodate both craft in passing, but I skirted even further than necessary to the right to avoid the salt and sand in his wake. I wondered whether Tillvan planned to avail himself of public transportation upon his arrival.

Upon reaching Sayoun, I swung down a sideway that took me around behind *The Silver Pestle*. There I docked, and ascended the wrought-iron steps to the fire door. Once again it opened soundlessly. I cracked it enough to see that the hallway was empty, and quickly ducked inside. At any moment Silver LeMay might emerge from her room or climb the stairs from the deli. The telltales on and around my door and sensor pad had not been disturbed. Opening the door, I rolled inside and came up with the Stern sweeping the room. As was the case in ninety-nine out of a hundred entries, the precautions proved baseless.

After the customary search I scooped up the ashtray from the nightstand, sat down at the table in front of the window, drew the curtains, and made myself comfortable with the flask of Knockando and a cheroot while the evening fell outside. I sat there for perhaps an hour, drifting, drinking, and smoking, before I allowed my thoughts to range toward Silver LeMay.

Despite the attacks at the beach and the cove, despite her innuendos of a relationship, LeMay remained my first choice as the threat to Tillvan. Her skill with weapons of all types gave her the means, and the contract from Ecotect gave her the motive. She could easily avail herself of a suitable opportunity. She was possessed of the coldness necessary to dispatch her target and to accept the occurrence of violent death, as she had demonstrated in the foothills near the cove. She was, in short, too much like me.

But it was impossible for me to escape the innuendoes and the hints, some more blatant than others. In those moments she seemed on the verge of, as they say, making an offer. Yet she knew who I was, and given that her target was Tillvan, she surely understood why I was in Sayoun. Or perhaps she found my assignment incredible; we are not known for keeping people alive. If so, perhaps she thought we were competitors after all, going after the same target. That would explain her remark about lionesses hunting.

I made a sound of disgust and fired up another cheroot. It seemed that any image I might have of Silver LeMay as a lover was overwhelmed by professional considerations. In my mind she might be tender or deadly, but not both. And at this moment I wanted to envision her as tender.

Why?

I tilted the flask and discovered that it was empty.

Why?

Admit it!

I started to light another cheroot and realized that I already had one going.

Silver . . . Diana . . .

She knew we were potential adversaries, yet rather than attempt to eliminate me, she made overtures. Why? Operatives like myself and mortifices like her employ friendship as a weapon. For us, deceptions are tools of our respective trades, trust is a blunt instrument, sex is misdirection. She knew that. She knew that I knew that. So why make the overture?

Why?

Because she meant it.

It kept coming back to that, overriding my objections. The evidence went beyond hints and inklings and suggestions. She possessed an art collection she was so far unable to share. She had received complicated missions, and supposed that I had as well. *Don't you just hate that kind of assignment?* She had revealed an innermost desire in wanting to see the next tomorrow. Calculatedly, perhaps, but it was also true beyond her ability as an actor to express. It was an exposure of her soul.

I could retire here.

We're not expected to outlive them.

I'm safe, I had told Deven. Who else can she talk shop with?

Who else can I talk shop with?

I decided not to dry the single tear that spilled down the right side of my nose. It could not possibly exist. Emotions are an operative's bane. We hide them away, to be released only during nightmares. So I could not have shed a tear. In Blacklight Section, logic is simple and direct. Don't feel, just go there, and kill that.

Kill Silver LeMay.

If I could locate her, I would do so. I was thinking that perhaps I should start by looking in the Andromeda Galaxy when I heard a knock on my door, four soft raps, the last one scarcely audible. It was a knock of the reluctant, or of the faint of heart.

Immediately I was on my feet, the Stern in my right hand, the cheroot now smoldering on top of the nightstand, having missed the ashtray. From the bed I seized a pillow and covered my mouth with it, and took up a position beside the door.

"Who is it?" I called.

The voice that replied was faint, and taut with pain. "Are you *M'selle* Nyx? I-I need to speak with you . . . "

Relief that the caller was not LeMay irritated me, but the voice itself put me on edge. If not LeMay, then who? "Keep your hands empty and in plain sight," I said. I gave her a count of five and threw the door open in the recommended manner.

As tall as LeMay, the girl standing before me was slender without being frail. She might have been as old as eighteen. She held her arms at her sides, empty palms toward me. She was wearing the pants to an emerald green leisure suit with the drawstring tied in a bow just to the left of center, and a bandeau of fabric of the same color held in place by insewn elastic bands above and below her fist-sized breasts. Her feet were bare and sandy. Her cap of jet black was just long enough to reach her eyebrows and the nape of her neck. Large green eyes dominated her face, and her underlying tan was showing signs of fresh sunburn. Dried tears streaked her face, and her thin lips were still wet from blubbering.

The girl did not appear to notice the Stern in my hand.

"She said," she began, and stopped, and tried again. "She said you were there when Agate was . . . killed. She said you would tell me what happened . . . "

"Step inside, please."

She did so, trudging uncertainly. After I closed the door, I ordered

63

her to lean forward against the wall, legs apart, hands flat.

"Wh-what for?" she asked.

"I'm going to search you," I said. "Your only other choice is to leave."

Her voice regained some of its strength. "She told me you could be cruel."

"The wall, if you please?"

When she was in position, I patted her down for weapons, and found only a PHL in the right front pocket of her suit pants. Her body had the firmness of a runner, and callouses on her hands bespoke bouts of long hard work. I made a mental note not to underestimate her.

"All right, Kitch," I said. "Turn around, and sit down on the bed."

She seated herself warily. "You know my name?"

"There's no one else you could be," I told her. "Under the circumstances. Which I wish were different, believe me."

With that, Kitch began to weep. She had already gone through that body-wracking cry of total grief, and had little strength left for anguish. For a moment I felt a sense of loss. I had seen others emotionally destroyed, but never experienced it myself. I sat down beside her on the bed and put an arm around her shoulders, trying gently to draw her closer. She resisted this, but did not pull away. I felt mechanical, as if the comfort I offered was perfunctory, and perhaps it was. I was going through what seemed to be the proper motions of consolation.

"What happened?" whispered Kitch.

I kept it simple and detached. "Diana and I flew to the cove just to see it. Nothing more sinister than that. Agate followed us. She wanted to talk. She said that she would stop us from exploiting the coastline. She seemed to think that we, on behalf of AmResCor, would use the excuse of the murder on the beach yesterday of a corporate official to start killing Ecotect protesters--as a pre-emptive measure or perhaps in retaliation. We . . . did not have time to assure her that this was not our purpose. Agate was shot from behind at long range. She died instantly."

"She was *murdered*!" Kitch cried.

"Yes, Kitch."

She turned her freckled face toward me, her eyes wet and glowing. "And nothing happened to you at all!"

"Diana and I---"

"*Nothing at all!*"

"Please let me finish, Kitch."

"Why didn't they shoot you too?" she said hotly.

"Diana and I took cover behind a some boulders on a hillock, Kitch. Agate's killer came after us. We waited until he was within range, and we killed him, she and I. He is dead."

Kitch stared down at the floor, at her sandy toes. Maybe she had heard what I had said, maybe she was thinking about Agate. Her face was slack, impossible to read. Her tears continued to flow, but she was no longer aware of them. Again I felt a sense of loss, without knowing what it was I had lost. Perhaps I had never had it.

"That explains it," whispered Kitch.

"What's that?"

"About an hour ago. The Constable and his men brought in two airfoils. One had been badly broken up. There were two bodies, in--in bags. One was Agate, I heard one of the constables saying that. It's the girl called Agate, he said, with Ecotect. But that explains why they brought in so much more than . . . Agate. I wanted to see . . . see her, but they know me."

"Did you happen to hear anyone mention the name of the other person they brought in?" I asked.

She shook her head. "I don't remember. Maybe . . . I remember thinking, that's an opera."

"You had more important things on your mind," I said gently. "I understand."

With that, Kitch collapsed against me. I thought she was going to break down again, but she hardly moved except for a sniffle to clear her nose. I felt wooden. Deven does not train operatives to relieve grief. Quite the opposite. At the moment, words failed me. Whatever I might say was either the wrong thing or irrelevant. I kept my arm around her, ready to release her if that's what she wanted, and waited.

The very last thing I expected was another knock on my door, but it came, a staccato of five raps this time, evenly spaced. The damn room was getting more attention than a Spaceport Terminal. I reacquired the pillow and asked for identification.

"It's me," said LeMay.

I dropped the pillow and, against all training, leaned against the door. I felt a weakness greater than exhaustion. I was already depressed when Kitch had showed up. In her presence, it had been a struggle to maintain a professional equilibrium. Now even that seemed lost to me. My knees buckled, and I almost fell.

"Go away, Diana."

My voice sounded strange to me, thick and constricted. LeMay detected this. "Are you okay?" she asked.

I swore, and forced myself upright. "Diana, please. I *cannot* see you. *Please!*"

"Nyx, you sound---"

"*Go away!*"

I did not hear her response, nor did I hear her retreating footsteps. Presently I returned to the bed and to Kitch. I felt heartsick. I was under strict orders to feel no such thing, but Deven wasn't here. Eventually, if I survived this mission, I would have to report my thoughts, feelings, and experiences. Determining what I could get away with omitting was going to be a task indeed.

Meanwhile, there was a girl beside me who had felt a loss I had never known. As I put my arm around her again, she leaned into me. She had stopped crying. She did whimper once, and then was still. At length she withdrew a little and looked at me. "I thought you and she were---" she began, and paused, the next word pregnant in the air between us.

We're not, I started to say. We should be, I wanted to say. What I managed to get out was, "This isn't about me right now, Kitch. This is about you."

"It's about both of us, I think," said Kitch. She gave me another unfathomable look, then turned and slid upon the bed, her left hand reaching for the pillow I had dropped on the floor. At last she stretched out on her back, and found a comfortable depression in the pillow for her head. "I just need to be held," she said, closing her eyes. "Just for a while."

And she was a comfort to cling to, to keep from drowning.

007

Sometime before dawn Kitch departed. Her movements awoke me, but I sensed the time for words had not reached us. In the event, she bent and kissed my temple, and slipped like a fog from the room, having received whatever she had needed from me. After a moment, I got up and secured the door, and went back to bed.

By the time morning arrived I had dozed fitfully for a while, and otherwise lain in bed, swatting random thoughts away. Deep in the background hovered a face framed by long, pale yellow hair. If I shut my eyes hard enough, the phosphorus sparks obscured that face. But it hurt too much to keep them shut.

Too restless now even to think about sleep, I got up and indulged in a leisurely shower, dug out fresh clothing--a light blue, spaghetti-strap top, if you must know, and black denims, with the bush hat tucked into a back pocket--and finally set the telltales inside the room and exited out the fire escape. The day was young, but maybe one of the kiosks had opened. Only a few people were about, one for an early morning jog, his round face already red with effort. He was older than I ever expected to be. Or Silver expected--but it was far too early in the day for that kind of morbidity. An urchin in the back of my mind asked, what other kind of morbidity is there? It was enough to stop me from frowning.

With a weather eye out for Silver LeMay, I made for the kiosk I had visited yesterday and found the attendant there fussing with the folding panels that covered the window. He had a routine and was sticking to it despite the arrival of a prospective customer. Wire racks with little bottles of liquor in place. Confectionaries next, in slanted slotted shelving. Packages of dried fruit and nuts, and other munchies. Vials of scents and washes and sprayshoe and sunblock, little tins of body tints, bottles of eyeliner and henna. Everything in its own place. If you carry enough different products, you're bound to sell something. The attendant was about my age, in his middle to late twenties, a short and wiry man with streaked brown hair and a beach tan, and dressed in brown. His economy of movement during set-up suggested that he had been doing this for years. The edge of weariness in his blue eyes said that he might be doing this for the rest of his life.

"Ready?" I asked, after he climbed into the kiosk and stood behind the counter.

He shook his head. "Not for another half-hour."

I heaved an exaggerated sigh. "I suppose I can wait another thirty minutes. I wouldn't want you to violate any ordnances."

He straightened a display that did not appear to need it. "It's not that, so much," he said. A hint of bitterness crept into his tone. "But after yesterday, the constables are going to be watching. It's okay for people like us to get killed, but when it happens to a constable, they---"

"What happened yesterday?"

He shot me a questioning look. "You didn't hear?"

"I was on a tour."

He looked as if he were not sure he should be discussing the events. Resignation made him grimace. "There have been two constables killed in the past two days," he told me. "They're down to eight now, although I suppose they could hire---"

"Wait. The man killed yesterday was a constable?"

"That's what I heard, yes."

"You wouldn't happen to know his name." The attendant shook his head, and I went on, "You were going to say?"

"Hmm? Oh, right, they could hire some of the old ones back if they had to."

"What old ones?"

"The constables that worked Sayoun before the present group arrived, about twenty days ago," said the attendant tolerantly. "They're in Makalla now. That's about a hundred kilometers out Sayoun, north, on the coast. The people are mostly retirees and expatriates from Siena, Italy. A few stragglers." He paused, and made a face at the world. "I don't ever remember anyone being killed here, not until this. I've been here all my life, twenty-two years, and never--I mean, this is a peaceful place. Boring, but peaceful. Or it was."

"You know for certain the old constables are in Makalla?" I asked.

"That's what they say, yes."

I glanced furtively around me. I always assume I'm being watched, but in this instance the possibility of surveillance felt almost claustrophobic. I really did not want to spot a tall, slender woman with long, pale yellow hair, but I had no doubt whatsoever that she was around somewhere. I found nothing amiss, except the jogger I had passed earlier, who was now florid upon his return. I hoped he would not keel over dead, and attract a constable.

"If I promise not to tell anyone, would you please sell me a bag of that trail mix and . . . " I looked over the liquor offerings, and dug out my flask. "And three little bottles of Jura?"

He cracked a smile and passed me the trail mix. "I have a half-liter of Jura in stock below," he told me, arching one bushy brown eyebrow.

"Even better."

He produced the bottle, and I was pleased to see that it was glass. The plastic of the little ones tends to alter the taste of the contents.

"AV55," he said. I peeled off a hundred-note, and he gave me change. "That's not much of a breakfast," he pointed out.

"I'm saving the trail mix for lunch," I said.

Following a circuitous route I made for my airfoil behind *The Silver Pestle*, and after ascertaining that it had not been tampered with overnight, I boarded up. Assuming Silver LeMay was conducting surveillance on foot, she would now be eager to reach her own craft, but I did not notice anyone rushing about in the periphery. Of course, LeMay also might still be in bed. I quickly quashed that imagery, powered up, and swung the airfoil to the main glideway, banking west for the coast.

After reaching the limits of Sayoun, I turned north, following the same route LeMay and I had taken yesterday. This time, if necessary, I meant to travel considerably further. It was not necessary for me to travel at all, of course, provided that I could raise a constable in Makalla, but I also wanted to find out whether anyone would follow me. An abrupt and unannounced journey is a simple yet useful artifice to that end. After verifying that I had not yet acquired a tail, I dug out the Personal Holographic Link and had my 'skipcomp raise the Makalla Constabulary, or the equivalent.

"There is no Makalla Constabulary," Niobe informed me.

"Who keeps order there?"

"There is no one on official status."

The glideway vanished as I reached relatively flat and unobstructed terrain. I set the groundhug application at a meter-fifty, high enough to reduce the dust in my wake and, therefore, my visibility, and accelerated to 120. So far, I seemed to have the coastline to myself.

"And unofficially?" I asked Niobe.

"There is a paramedic and a fire station, co-located."

"Raise the paramedic, please."

Moments later I heard a voice, just audible over the gusts that rounded the plexishield. I increased the volume. "Say again all after?"

It was the creaky voice of a man somewhat advanced in years, speaking with a trace of accent. "My name isa Rigantonio. How may I helpa you?"

"Rigantonio?" I recalled something Kitch had said. "Isn't that an opera?"

"That'sa *Rigoletto.* Hey, you sounda like a young woman."

"My name is Nyx, *Signor* Rigantonio. I'm looking for some constables who may have moved to Makalla from Sayoun."

The silence that ensued was almost palpable, and for a moment I wondered whether he had rung off. When he spoke again, his voice sounded even older.

"May I ask, *per favore,* have you official status, *Signorina* Nyx?"

"If I need it."

I could feel him mull over the implications, though I had admitted to practically nothing.

"*Non c'e nessuno,*" he said at last. "There isa no one, officially. *Capisce?* You understand?"

Even a single word in another language can go a long way, can prove even more effective than AV100 notes. "*Capisco, Signore,*" I said. "*Dove sta?* Where are you?"

After receiving directions to the fire station, I broke commo, and then asked for a projection of the coastal topogram. Unfortunately, the download from Deven extended only halfway up the coast to Makalla, and Niobe's database had nothing to supplement the information, so I was unable to view the settlement itself. Reaching Makalla was a simple enough task; all I had to do was bear north along the coast. Justifying the trip as a mission requirement was another matter. I was not on Adenne to play hunches. I was here to keep one Ashler M. Tillvan alive--almost an impossible task for a solitary operative--but for how long? Deven had not been specific in that regard. The tasking had originated outside Blacklight. If a time limit had been set, Deven would have informed me. Therefore, it had not been set, or at least Deven had not been told about it, and he is loathe to tolerate open-ended missions. In our line of work, tasking is expected to be conclusive, if you see what I mean.

I sighed. Whatever happened to go there and kill that?

In fact, I did have such an order, one that I was disobeying, or at best avoiding. I disabled the topogram and realized I was passing just west of the hillock where LeMay and I had dispatched Agate's killer. Flashes of reflected sunlight caught my eye, and I swung the airfoil east and brought it to hover at the base of the western slope. Grenke's people had missed a few pieces of debris in front of the boulders that clustered at the crest of the hillock, and a few of them now glistened. A brown smear on the sand indicated where Agate had fallen. Alerted by a sudden chill between my shoulder blades, I threw a glance toward the ocean, but no one had risen from the cove to shoot at me. To the south, however, roiled a wake of sand and dust.

It was too late to hide. Headlong flight was an option, but Deven prefers that this be performed directly at the target. I set the airfoil down and pulled out the Krupp Stern. LeMay's Ecko had me by five meters of range, but if I could somehow evade her first beam, she might pull within my range before she got off a second one. Or perhaps she would be content merely to heave to at fifty meters and invest me with harsh language. If I survived this, Deven was going to assign me to desk ops for the next five years, for not carrying out a direct order. At the moment, I could hardly fault him.

The airfoil gradually came into focus and seemed to be slowing. Its colors were red and gold, but something was wrong on the bridge. The hair of the operator was not long and pale yellow, as I had been hoping to see and not to see, but short and intensely black.

"Kitch," I muttered, but did not put the Stern away. Whoever had killed Terreme on the beach had fled in a red and gold airfoil. While there might be a hundred such craft of that color on Adenne, sooner or later one of them would be carrying a hostile operator, and as grieving and forlorn as Kitch had been last night, there was no reason for me to suppose that her intentions now were amicable.

Kitch drew up smoothly off my port bow, and cut the fans to dock down, oblivious to the Stern in my hand and the tension in my face and shoulders. She had changed from her emerald green outfit to a cropped sleeveless top and loose cotton shorts, both deep blue. The front of the top was emblazoned with a small color print of the cove a kilometer to our west. Her smile of greeting ended abruptly as she came to realize exactly where she was. With a little cry of anguish she dismounted and ran to the smear on the sand, and dropped to her knees.

I put the Stern away and joined her there, careful not to intrude into her grief. Tears spilled from the tip of her nose onto the sand, and her lips formed words that I was unable to hear. Gently she pushed sand over the dried blood of her lover, and covered that sand with an array of stones to mark the site.

When at last Kitch stood up, her face appeared as I had seen it the night before: tear-streaked, with lips wet, and glistening now in the sunlight. I had no words for her. When she drew abreast of me, she said, without looking at me, "You didn't lead me here on purpose."

"Had I known you were there, Kitch, I would have led you away."

She gave a little nod. "I'm glad you didn't. At least I got to . . . " She paused, and glanced back at the little pile of stones. "I can't get to her," she whispered. "It's not safe. I can't . . . care for her ashes, I can't . . . "

"Kitch." She shrugged away when I touched her shoulder, and started to board back up. "Why are you following me, Kitch?"

"I'm not. I had to leave Sayoun," she explained. "Noone said they were looking for me. They think I killed him . . . that constable."

"But you didn't."

Kitch took my statement for a question. "No! No, of course not."

"So why north? Where are you headed, Kitch?"

"To Makalla. Three others in our group are already there. The constables want to get rid of all of us now." Kitch gave me a sidelong glance. "Why are you asking so many questions?" Green eyes wide with sudden fear, she backed away. "Are you with the Constabulary? Or security? Oh, you *are*! Oh, no!"

I lunged, and grabbed her right arm above the elbow as she turned to flee. She tore my hand loose and twisted my arm, intending to apply leverage to ride me to the ground, and I recalled having made a mental note regarding her fitness. I leaned and turned into her grasp and threw her over my left hip and onto her back. She lay stunned, and I gave her no time to recover. She blinked, staring up at the Stern in my hand.

"*Damn it!*" I exploded. "Do you have any idea what I am supposed to do, what I am *trained* to do, if attacked? D'you get that, Kitch? This isn't some adolescent protest game you're playing now. You're among grown-ups, and if you lose at this level, it's *forever*."

"So *kill me* then," she cried. "Just do it."

I dropped to a knee beside her, and jammed the Stern against her throat. "I can do exactly that, Kitch," I assured her, more calmly now. "I can do it, and the outfit I work for will wrap it all up with a pretty red ribbon and nobody will ask any questions, ever. Here lies Kitch, dead because she tried to take on a pro." I got up, and yanked her to her feet. She stood rubbing her throat, eyes filled with defiance and an inner resolve that had not been present before. "Did you get any of that?" I asked her.

Kitch spoke quietly. "You're angry because you are frightened."

"Because I was afraid I would be forced to kill you, Kitch," I pointed out. I put the Stern away. "And you're a little young to have that kind of intuition."

"How old do I have to be?"

I met her gaze briefly, and nodded. "Move your airfoil behind this hill, where it's unlikely to be seen, and then board up with me. I'm headed for Makalla myself, and I'll get you there safely."

"Okay." She hesitated, and looked at me sharply. "Suppose I just take off on you. What happens then?"

"Then, unlike the constables, you'll be alone and unarmed."

Kitch licked her lips, which were beginning to dry in the sunlight. "I'll just be a moment," she said, and boarded her airfoil.

For perhaps ten minutes Kitch rode with me in silence on the bridge. She seemed to be staring at some point beyond the edge of the universe, and I reckoned she was reminiscing about Agate. From time to time her shoulders trembled with the intensity of a particular memory. In other moments, they slumped dejectedly. Whatever flashbacks she recalled were real, and the emotional responses she made to them were genuine. That sense of loss returned to me. My emotional responses might be contrived at will. Sometimes it was difficult to separate them from what I truly felt. The outburst of anger I had displayed when Kitch had attacked me was real enough, as were the words I had used to express it. Yet I was also trying to impress her, so that I wouldn't be forced to kill her unnecessarily at some point in the future. How much of it, then, was real, and how much contrived? And if I succeeded in impressing her, did it really matter?

"You're deep in thought," said Kitch.

I started. "Here I was, thinking the same with regard to you."

"I miss her," she said simply.

"She had courage," I said. "She thought we were from security, and yet she stood up to us."

Kitch nodded, but offered no comment.

"How long have you been protesting for Ecotect?" I asked her.

The question seemed to take her by surprise, but she answered readily enough. "About three years now. Agate and I were attending a lyceum on Jalune. Word got around among the students that

Amphictyony Products Corporation was sloughing a chemical slag into one of the rivers, and fish were disintegrating, and swimmers had their flesh fall off. So I joined a protest." She paused, and shivered at some memory. "We actually met at a rally. She said my name was too long, so she shortened it to Kitch."

"What is your name, then?"

"McKittrick Day. I was named for my father's and mother's families."

I recognized the name from the list the Emmix lot attendant had provided me. In theory she now became a prime suspect in Terreme's murder, but I didn't believe it for a second. "Kitch is easier on the tongue," I conceded. "So what happened at the rally?"

"The authorities came and broke it up, not very gently. My father had to pay a marker and assure the magistrate that I would behave myself."

"And did you?"

Kitch just laughed.

"A lyceum," I repeated. "How old are you?"

"Seventeen. Agate and I are . . . were . . . oh, fuck!"

I gave her a moment, and said, "I'm sorry."

Kitch shook her head almost violently. "You didn't mean to," she said, her voice hoarse with pain. At length she stood up straight, legs braced, shoulders squared. "I will," she said, but she was addressing someone I could not see. Following a long pause, she went on, "We were advanced students, with a strong academic background. I'll return to Jalune University next semester. I'm a third-year botany major, and Agate . . . " She swallowed hard, and stopped.

"Mineralogy?" I guessed.

Kitch nodded. "Her real name is . . . was Agatha. She was working on a process of using monochromal photonic resonance in specific wavelengths to identify concentrations of various elements and minerals deep in the mantles of planets, based on some experimental work that had already been done. Of course, identification is not extraction, but she always said you had to start someplace." Her voice trailed off with, "You have to start someplace . . . "

"Kitch?"

"She thought . . . Agate thought that at some point technology would develop to extract useful minerals from deep underground with minimal damage to the local ecology, and that her identification process would assist in this." She paused, and her face contorted in bitter anguish. "But of course AmResCor doesn't even bother to protect the ecology when the damn minerals are practically on the surface of the ground. Am I boring you?" she snapped. "You keep looking around."

"I get nervous when people follow me."

She whirled around. "We're being followed?" she cried.

"I haven't spotted anyone, no."

We were approaching a point where the chain of foothills bent to the west, to jut out into the ocean as a series of islets. As we were bearing directly north, we had to weave our way along the valleys and saddles. This limited our straight-line visibility, and a tail could take advantage of that and close with us, perhaps even enough so to mount an attack. But Kitch's expression was grim and determined after I explained these circumstances to her, and she kept hard watch aft while I got us through the chain unscathed.

Some twenty minutes later we emerged onto a savannah that began just inland of the shore, which was visible to us now because the escarpment had ended where the chain of hills met the ocean. Evidently the chain marked the boundary of a slightly different climate. Though the ground looked sandy, it contained enough soil to support a groundcover that varied in density here and there, and vast patches of knee-high turquoise grass. Trees were more abundant here, though still misshapen by the winds off the ocean. This terrain stretched inland as far as I could see, and appeared to be even more fertile in the distance, with clusters of trees interrupting the horizon.

I was thinking that here it was more idyllic than the cove when I caught a flash of movement well off to the west. In that same moment, Kitch crammed her fist against her mouth to stifle a cry.

"I see it," I said, and fished the utility bin for binox. "Take the helm," I told her, as we switched sides on the bridge, "and hold it steady."

Through the binox I saw a powder blue airfoil hurtling south along the beach, above the wet sand to minimize a detectable wake. I reckoned her speed at over 150. Already we had passed one another, and I had to continuously adjust the focus as we separated, but I was able to identify the operator as Associate Constable Frazier. He did not appear to have spotted us.

"Him," said Kitch, when I told her. "He's attended our meetings recently."

I felt a *frisson* of concern, but decided to withhold it from Kitch. "You sound a bit chilly," I said, as I regained the helm.

"Oh, he has stood up with us," she told me. "He says all the right things."

"But you doubt his sincerity."

Kitch made a face, her lower lip covering her upper. "Well, he *is* a constable," she said. "But he seemed to be trying to find a middle ground between his work and his off-duty activities. Seemed to be," she repeated.

"But you doubt his sincerity," I pressed.

"Agate told me she thought he had joined us to try to get laid."

"Ah. I understand."

"The problem was, Agate and I are . . . the only females in the group, at least until others arrive. It did not seem to occur to him that no today also meant no tomorrow."

"You didn't miss all that much," I said dryly.

Kitch turned to stare at me. "You?"

"In my line of work, you take what you can get when you can get it," I said. "But I have to admit, I could have done without it."

"I thought you and she--that woman---."

"Can we not discuss her right now, please?"

"Sorry," said Kitch. "Is she in your line of work, too?"

"Damn it, Kitch---"

"Sorry. Again."

Who else can I talk shop with?

I sighed. I could not divulge much to Kitch. On the other hand, she was here, with me. I said, "Yes. Generally, yes, she is. But we don't work for the same people."

"And you--you kill people?" When I did not reply, she went on, "You don't have to answer. I get it. *M'selle* Nyx?"

"Just Nyx."

She licked her lips nervously, steeling herself for the question. "Are you here to kill someone?"

"My primary mission is to keep someone alive," I said, which was the better half of it.

Kitch nodded, thinking. "So you and that woman---"

"Diana."

"Yes, Diana . . . are arguing, and you are both in the same line of work. Which means *she's* here to kill someone." Her eyes grew huge with realization. "She's here to kill the person you're supposed to keep alive! Of course!" Then: "*Oh, no!*"

"What is it?"

"She's here--Diana is here to kill my father!"

"Who's your father?"

"Ashler Tillvan."

I chuckled. "That's who I'm supposed to protect. Ashler M. Tillvan." I glanced at her sharply. "How is he your father?"

"Ashler McKittrick Tillvan."

008

I won't say that Kitch's revelation clarified the scenario for me, but it did shed some light on one or two matters. Kitch was not likely to convert this assignment to a Greek tragedy by killing her father. That was someone else's role. But whose? Diana's, just possibly, but the deeper I examined that theory, it weakened, despite Kitch's justifiable concerns. Given that Diana had been contracted by Ecotect, Tillvan could well be her target, but if so, then Diana, knowing who I was, should have tried to kill me at the earliest possible opportunity, regardless of her remark about lionesses.

I must have growled in frustration, because Kitch asked, "What was that for?"

"I was just wondering why I was still alive."

Her jaw dropped. "What an odd thing to say."

"This entire mission has been odd."

Kitch reached across the bridge and touched my arm. "It involves my father," she said quietly. "Let me help."

"This isn't . . . "

"It isn't a child's game," she finished for me. "Well, my lover has been murdered, my father is about to be murdered, and I'm riding along with a murderer. Just how grown up do I have to be?" She made a sudden sound of anguish. "I'm sorry. That was a bit harsh."

"What you have to understand, Kitch, is that your assessment of me is accurate. Plus it's dangerous to be around me."

"I believe you. Let me help."

Well, I had warned her. In point of fact, I was already mulling over the possibility of using her. To protect Tillvan I needed a team, and Kitch might well possess vital information about him. If it became necessary to place her in harm's way to fulfill my mission, that was too bad for Kitch. But Deven allows us a little leeway, to make such placements unnecessary, if we can.

"There's Makalla," announced Kitch.

What I saw was a horizon of irregularly-spaced bungalows of prefab wood and asphalt tile roofing, in yards whose boundaries were marked by what looked like low hedgerows. Most of the yards contained fruit and olive trees and flowers, and a few of them displayed concrete statuary. Makalla looked, in brief, like a small settlement of individual retirement homes, and occupied by, as the kiosk attendant had said, people from Italy, which explained Rigantonio's accent.

A block-like structure on the west side of Makalla rose above the others: the fire station, readily visible as Rigantonio had assured me. I banked the airfoil toward it. We had yet to acquire a tail, but that failed to reassure me. Silver LeMay was skillful enough to remain unseen--or to already be in place in Makalla. After my terse dismissal at the *Pestle* and the rejection later that evening, I had no clue as to her state of mind.

I also had to wonder what Associate Constable Frazier, late of my boudoir, had been doing so far north of Sayoun. A village of retirees and expatriates hardly seemed the type to appeal to him, although he need not have come all this way, of course. Perhaps Makalla fell within the jurisdiction of the Constabulary. Still, his visit was a factor to keep in mind.

We reached the fire station without obstruction. Of brick construction, and with a roof that slanted to the rear to keep the rain off the entrance, it looked strong enough to anchor the rest of the village. Battlements around the top of the station even suggested a castle, although they were as useless as Doric columns on a pagoda. A great tree grew near the right front corner of the building, festooned with deep blue fruit, perhaps a variety of plum. A few of its smaller branches had wedged themselves under the tiles at the edge of the roof. Something scurried between the feeder roots as we docked down.

A door in the side of the fire station had been emblazoned with a red cross. Kitch and I entered, and found ourselves in a dimly-lit and slightly musty hallway that passed along three doors. The last of them was ajar.

Rigantonio rose and moved from behind his desk to greet us when we stepped into his office. Well into his second century, he was older than I had supposed, but the gray-green eyes on either side of a bulbous, rosacea-scarred nose retained much from his youth. He had reached the age where a young woman on his arm gave him cachet among his peers, and in that sense he regarded us hungrily. He stood about a head shorter than Kitch, and he was wearing a white shirt under blue bib dungarees, black boots, and a white paramedic's jacket, all freshly cleaned. I wondered whether he had changed clothes just for us. About him was none of that elderly male smell, only a sweetish, inexpensive body scent, too much of which he had undoubtedly applied in the last several minutes. I had no trouble at all finding a smile for him, and if he wanted to look us over, surely his long years of helping others warranted that as a reward. A glance at Kitch told me she was also taken by him. She seemed to know her sexuality was perfectly safe among his memories.

After we introduced ourselves, Rigantonio's expression lost some of its sparkle. "Maybe sometime you come backa for a longer visit, eh?" he said, and sobered. "Thisa bad business, *Signorina* Nyx, *Signorina* Kitch. After I receive-a you commo, I move-a him here, so you can-a see."

He led us from the office with a, "You come," and took us to the middle door. His wrinkled face was sad now, the crow lines on the outside corners of his eyes more marked, as he gently pushed the door open. Beside me, Kitch caught her breath, then gasped.

In the center of what was clearly a first-aid and medical treatment room room sat a man in a straight wooden chair, facing us. Ordinary in appearance, he was perhaps in his late thirties. He was attired in a white medical gown that reached to his ankles. Hard-worn blue slippers shod his feet. His face bore signs of a recent beating, and the last two fingers on his left hand were bound together with medical tape.

His face was completely slack. He stared straight ahead, unblinking, as if we were not there.

"This-a Associate Constable Hokins," Rigantonio said softly, his accent now far more pronounced. "Fifteen days ago, he broughta his-a friends onna airfoil, much-a like yours. They were dead. He was almost-a dead. I don'ta know how he got them here. Physically he could not have-a done it. He put-a the airfoil down. He . . . I hide-a him at-a my

79

home, and-a bury his-a friends, five friends-a. All dead. All-a beaten."
Rigantonio looked up at me, tears in his eyes. "I can-a do nothing more
for him. You help-a, *sí*? You help-a him, *signorina*, *per piacere*, please-a,
you help-a him."

"There's nothing I can do, *Signor* Rigantonio," I said. "Maybe I can
make contact with someone. That's about all."

"Anything, *piacere*, *signorina*."

"Do you know who did this to him?"

Rigantonio pulled at his lower lip, and shook his head. In a low
voice, Kitch said, "There must be something we can do for him."

"We can discuss it later," I told her. "*Signor* Rigantonio, can you keep
him hidden for a few more days? Don't tell anyone else that he's alive or
that he's here."

He nodded vigorously. "Sure, sure, *certo*. He stay with-a me." The
glimmer of hope in his eyes said he was misreading my purpose. I was
thinking that silence would help keep them both alive.

I tugged at Kitch, and she came with me reluctantly. As we boarded
the airfoil, Rigantonio gave us a little forlorn wave from the side door.
Perhaps he had grasped that no help was in the offing. It was easy to tell
myself that this was not my concern. Certainly the assistance he
required did not fall anywhere near the scope of my duties. I could even
hear Deven's dry voice chiding me for sentimentality. Still, rules were
made to be circumvented; I just had to go about it the right way.

"They're in the last bungalow," said Kitch, pointing, as I guided the
airfoil onto the glideway that split Makalla on its way to the shore. After
a moment she pulled out her PHL and began to transmit a code. I closed
my hand around it and yanked it from her grasp.

"We'll be there presently," I said. "Whatever you have to say can
wait."

Kitch glowered at me, but tucked the PHL into her pocket when I
returned it to her.

The tension between us made it difficult to enjoy a few moments of
tranquility as we passed between the rows of bungalows. A few older
folks labored out in the sunlight, trimming this and pruning that, or
picking fruit and olives, while others sat on patios and porches. An
intermittent breeze from the ocean carried strains of music from one of
the dwellings, along with faint aromas of brine and decomposition from
the beach, and now and then a dog barked. Beside me, Kitch stood with

her back stiff. Finally she pointed to the last bungalow on the right, not far from a strip of sparse grassland that separated the village from the beach, and I drew the airfoil up and docked her.

As soon as we touched down Kitch tried to disembark, but I held her back. Already I had noticed that the front door was open, and hanging from only the top hinge. "Stay here," I told her, and stepped down, Stern in hand. A warning glance back at Kitch froze her in the act of trying to follow. I hoped I had gotten through to her. It's difficult enough to enter a potentially hostile environment without having to account for unwanted assistance.

Crossing the yard from the airfoil to the front door left me vulnerable, but I kept my profile low and dodged from side to side, as I had been taught, until I pulled up beside the door. A quick peek inside told me only that two rattan patio chairs had been tossed about like rubbish. Nothing inside the house emitted a sound. I drew a steadying breath, and ducked inside in the prescribed manner.

The interior consisted of one main room, with alcoves for cooking, hygiene, and storage. Through the doorway I had only seen the right front quadrant of this room. My roll had carried me behind one of the rattan chairs, not the best of cover, but the room was empty of threats. Whoever was responsible for the three bodies on the floor by the cooking alcove had already departed.

A shadow appeared in the doorway, and I almost fired, then swore violently. "I told you to stay on the airfoil," I snapped.

Kitch was beyond hearing me. Her eyes were huge as she stared at the bodies, and behind her fist she was mewling. She took several little steps into the room. Then her knees buckled, and she sank to the floor, getting her hands down just in time to protect her face from impact.

She remained on hands and knees, gasping and crying, while I checked the three bodies, all young males. Two of them looked familiar, and I recalled having seen them in *The Bantam Cock*; the girl with them then had been Agate, I realized now. From their positions, I reckoned the killer or killers had burst into the bungalow and simply opened fire before anyone could escape. Two of the bodies had multiple burns from energy weapons. The third had a single scorched spot in the back, which he had evidently received as he rushed to the side window. I knelt beside him to feel his body temperature. It seemed to be just below normal, but above room temperature. I estimated they had been killed within the past hour.

Frazier, I thought, recalling that we had passed him on the coast heading back south.

Kitch regained her feet. On unsteady legs she leaned back against the wall by the door, shaking her head slowly in disbelief. Her eyes shot me a question.

"I'm not sure," I told her. "This doesn't make sense. You don't kill those who aren't a threat to you, unless their deaths have a specific purpose in your overall plan." I glanced at her sharply. "Or unless there's something you haven't told me?"

With a visible effort Kitch found her voice. "We protest," she said. "That's all we do. We just protest."

I tried to ease her out the door, but she shrugged away. "There's nothing you can do for them now," I said. "And we don't need to be in here."

"I can't just---"

"We'll make arrangements," I told her. "But we won't do it from in here. Come on."

Her shoulders slumped, and she relented. When we reached the airfoil, she sat down on the grass, staring at the bungalow. I had to wonder about her stability. She had lost a lot of people close to her in a very short time. People have been known to collapse into puddings under much less pressure. I spoke her name softly, and she looked up at me with surprisingly dry eyes. "This has to stop," she said.

"Maybe Ecotect has moved beyond protests," I suggested. "We spoke earlier about Diana, and her work. Kitch, she was hired by Ecotect."

Kitch shook her head. "That can't be right. We don't--no, we would never kill anyone. We never have. We barricade, sure. We march. We shout and chant. But--but at most, we might throw things."

"Fruit and such."

"And eggs, maybe. But we aren't killers," she insisted. Her dark brows knit. "How do you know she was hired by Ecotect?"

"My source is unimpeachable, believe me. That's who's paying her."

"That just doesn't make any sense."

I dug out my PHL. "Kitch, I have to make contact with my boss. I'd rather you weren't visible in the hologram."

After she climbed aboard and sat down on one of the aft benches, I strolled out to the strip of grassland and fifty meters from the airfoil, and raised Deven. As always, he responded immediately. I had Niobe configure his hologram as one of Michelangelo's cherubs to protect his physical identity, and project him onto the grass alongside the glideway.

I was standing with my back to the open ocean, and the hologram of me that he was seeing in his office showed nothing but beach and a few trees. "I gather this is not an update regarding the status of Silver LeMay," he said.

"I have not yet located her, sir. Perhaps she anticipated your orders."

"Very well. Report."

I brought him up to date on events, including Rigantonio, Frazier, and the bodies in the bungalow, omitting only Kitch's relationship to Tillvan. "Constable Grenke pointed out that Ecotect had easier access to older weapons, such as rifles, than to energy weapons," I added. "I don't know that this is true, but it's interesting that he could be trying to sway me in that direction. He suspects that I am associated in some way with professional security work. Perhaps he's setting me up to make an official report to this effect."

"I see. What do you think he hopes to gain by this?"

"Sir, it's going to depend on who killed whom why. Let's assume that a constable killed Manager Terreme. We know a constable killed Agate and tried to kill LeMay and me. Grenke's past record suggests that beating those five former constables to death would be his idea of a good time. And either LeMay or a constable killed the three young men here. I think once we understand the why, we'll know who."

"Nevertheless, Lieutenant, protecting Manager Tillvan remains your primary mission. The order regarding LeMay remains in effect."

"If LeMay did not in fact kill these three here," I countered, "she may not have killed anyone on Adenne at all, except in self-defense, which means it is entirely possible, even likely, that she is not here on a killing contract."

"Our tasking comes from AmResCor," Deven said severely. "I was not asked what I thought of it. If someone in that corporation is trying to be clever, compliance with orders may well serve to expose that individual."

I frowned at the cherub on the grass. Deven does not abide those who try to use Blacklight for their personal advantage, but he prefers to adhere to the literal words of tasking and let those who issued the orders stew in their own juices. Metaphorically, of course.

83

"If this clever individual wants Silver LeMay out of the way," I said carefully, "wouldn't it be to our advantage to keep her alive? Sir?"

Deven also chose his words. "What evidence do you have to indicate that she did not kill the three men in the bungalow?"

"I'm playing a hunch, sir."

"To be sure." He mulled this over for a few seconds, rubbing the tip of his nose with the first knuckle of his right index finger, a sure sign that he was disturbed. On a cherub, however, the gesture looked absurd, and I had to stifle a laugh. "Very well," he decided at last. "I shall pass on to AmResCor that Silver LeMay is no longer a factor. If she should become a factor again, your previous instructions regarding her are to be put into effect immediately."

"Yes, sir."

"In the meantime, I trust that she will remain invisible until you have satisfied your mission requirements. Which, by the way, are no longer open-ended. Manager Tillvan will make his own security arrangements once he has determined that a long-term presence needs to be established on Adenne. I am informed that two or three days will suffice for this."

"Understood, sir. Did you trace the Marlin?"

"It was reported stolen about fifty days ago from a private collection on Airwine, along with two boxes of ammunition. The case remains unsolved." The cherub looked at me sharply. "Yes, Lieutenant?"

"I recovered one box of shells with the Marlin," I told him. "He could have exhausted the other box while sighting in the rifle, I suppose, but I have to wonder whether maybe there's another rifle out there."

"I'll have Research go over reported recent thefts of Marlins. Perhaps they'll turn up something."

"Have them check on Model 1895 Remingtons and Springfields, too," I suggested. "They'll take that .444 cartridge as well. One more thing, sir. The dossier on Grenke in the Rec Room indicated that he was here on Adenne in an unknown capacity. Do we have any information regarding his whereabouts and activities immediately prior to his arrival?"

"If Research has anything, I'll pass it on. If that's all, Lieutenant?"

"Yes, sir." After the cherub faded, I returned to the airfoil and gave it a little jostle, startling Kitch. "It's safe now," I told her.

Her eyes darkened with accusation. "You said we would make arrangements."

"We'll stop by the fire station. Rigantonio will know what to do."

"There's a crematorium in Sayoun."

I swung myself aboard the airfoil and powered her up. "I don't think returning to Sayoun is a good idea right now. We'll speak with Rigantonio."

"And then what?"

I guided the craft back toward the fire station. "Who's Noone?" Kitch just looked at me, and I added, "You said he told you they were looking for you. They presumably being the constables. Is he Ecotect?"

Kitch gave a little cry of dismay, and grabbed her PHL. "I have to let him know," she said, and coded for him. "He attended our rallies, too. He's a costermonger in the park and on the beach."

"He's a what?"

"Sh!" She listened to a voice I could not make out clearly. "Kitch," she said, her voice shaking. "Stop what you're doing and leave Sayoun. Now."

"Have him come to Makalla," I said.

"Makalla," she repeated. "Come directly to . . . ," she looked at me.

"The fire station."

"The fire station, and try not to let anyone see you." I heard some garbled words, and then Kitch cried, "Because they're dead! They're all dead! Please, just get here, and be careful." After she closed commo, she looked at me with moist eyes. "He's working out at the beach right now. He'll head right up the coast."

"That should be safe enough," I said.

"That's not why I'm telling you."

I made a face. "No. I draw the line at escort duties."

"You can drop me off at the fire station."

"Dammit, Kitch---"

"*M'sieur* Rigantonio and I will work things out for . . . the others while you're gone."

"I am *not*---"

"Ah, we're here," said Kitch, and disembarked before I could complete my thought.

Which was just as well. After she gave me his description, I swung the craft around and made for the coast.

009

Under other circumstances a journey by airfoil along the west coast of Equatoria might have been a pleasant way to pass some time while on R&R on Adenne. In fact, I had been contemplating one or two such excursions before that first bullet struck the beach sand. As so often happens with the best plans of mice and men--and women--to get laid while on furlough, those plans had gone, as Robert Burns wrote, *a-gley*, that presumably being the Scottish word for "south." Which was the direction I was now headed.

The motive for killing the three young men in the Makalla bungalow remained obscure. As nearly as I could figure it, they posed no threat to anyone's plans--surely an apple cast at a corporate hierarch now and then can be dismissed. Yet killed they had been, and by someone who had done the deed dispassionately, with a detachment as cold as my own. Frazier, doubtless acting on orders from Grenke, seemed the obvious candidate, as Kitch and I had seen him heading south from Makalla on our way north.

I felt I was overlooking a significant factor in this mission. The further I traveled along the coastline, the more it nagged at me like a broken promise. Snatches of light fluttered in and out of my thoughts as I watched the waves tumble toward the shore. For a moment, I almost had it; then it eluded my grasp again. It was like trying to capture a butterfly while wearing boxing gloves. The missing factor had something to do with Frazier. But what was it?

The summary was simple enough. On orders from Grenke, Frazier flies to Makalla. He goes directly to the bungalow. He breaks down the door and kills three people with three bursts from an energy sidearm. It was not necessary to speak to them or argue with them. He then returns to Sayoun. While I might argue the necessity of the killings, I could respect the efficiency.

"What am I missing?" I snarled at the waves off the starboard bow of the airfoil.

I shook my head to clear it of the debris of logic and focused instead on when and where I might encounter Noone. Assume a journey of a hundred kilometers, the distance between Makalla and Sayoun. If one airfoil departs Makalla heading south at 150 kilometers an hour, and a second airfoil departs Sayoun heading north at 130 kilometers an hour, at what point will they meet? My education, like my childhood in the alleys of Smirk's Larder, had been intermittent. Whenever possible, I had snuck into the school and hung out in the rafters, eavesdropping on classes. Unfortunately, I had missed the lecture on math problems like this one. I could estimate, however, that Noone and I would meet at a point just south of midway between the two settlements. Given that he was not in enough hurry to push his craft to the max. Given that Frazier had not already overtaken him and killed him.

At the spot where the foothills ran out into the ocean and formed a chain of islets, where earlier Kitch and I had spotted Frazier, I slowed the airfoil in order to skirt the slope that jutted out into the waves. Salt spray flew up onto the plexishield, reducing visibility. To gain another two meters of clearance I adjusted the groundhug application, then banked out over the waves and around the slope. On the other side of it, for as far as I could see, the shoreline stretched along the ancient escarpment whose rupture had folded a section of crust into the chain of foothills. Slowing the airfoil to hover, I scanned the beach using the binox, but found no sign of Noone yet. Still, I was not necessarily alone on this stretch of coastline. I pulled the airfoil around the slope of the foothill, where it would not be noticed immediately by anyone coming round it from the north, and waited.

After ten minutes I had to conclude that either nobody was following me or whoever was following me now lurked on the other side of the foothill, having anticipated my defensive maneuver. If the latter, that person was now able to watch me leave without exposing her or his position. Since my departure from *The Silver Pestle* I had sensed that Silver LeMay was in my vicinity, though to what end I could not even begin to speculate. I recalled thinking, at the bungalow, that the killer had been cold and detached, relating those qualities to myself. But I had to concede that they also related to LeMay.

Two suspects, then. Armed and in the vicinity--assuming LeMay had been tailing me--both she and Frazier had means and opportunity. Only Frazier had an apparent motive: orders from Grenke. It seemed unlikely that Ecotect had hired LeMay to nock members of Ecotect . . . unless those members were about to embarrass the organization irreparably. Still, I felt I could almost eliminate LeMay as a suspect, because of the front door to that bungalow. Not that she was incapable of knocking a door off its hinges, but it wasn't her style. I mean, the noise alone would alert the occupants, and she would lose the element of surprise, as well as give them at least a tiny window of opportunity to escape. LeMay was a pro; she would not allow that.

On the other hand, Frazier, while not a pro, had surpassed amateur status. He had been vigilant in delivering me to the *Pestle*, and later that evening en route on foot to *The Bantam Cock*. Breaking down a door was not necessarily amateurish--if the intruder had help to cut off escape through the windows, for example--but it did complicate the reasoning.

Deven, of course, does not issue orders based on suspicion or speculation. Mine were clear: protect Ashler M. Tillvan until his security personnel were in place. I saw two ways to fulfill that mission. Protect him from those individuals of whom I was suspicious, or protect him from everyone. Fortunately, I still had the better part of two days to figure out which way I wanted to go with that.

Still alone on the coast, I set out once more toward the south, looking for Noone, who should have come into sight by now. In the distance rose the escarpment, broken where the cove bit into the coastline. The pale red afternoon sun flashed its light off the waves, and I had to shade my eyes to see. As the escarpment gradually drew away from the shore, allowing the beach to form, I altered course to pass over the wet sand, as Frazier had done, to minimize my own profile. Already I knew what I would find, given that I would find anything at all. I kept a weather eye out for wreckage, both on the shoreline and out in the water.

Birds ahead cued me. I hadn't seen many of them during my sojourn on Adenne, and certainly not a flock this size. Clusters of them soared overhead, each bird white with gray wings and about the size of a chicken. Around the rocks at the base of the escarpment within sight of the cove, another hundred or so had gathered. Sporadic fights had broken out to clarify positions in the pecking order, and now and then a loser fled, only to return to the group at some other point. On the rocks and sand beyond the main flock spread the debris of a shattered airfoil. Some of the fragments were red, some gold, others a bit of both.

As I approached, it became obvious that the birds were focused on a long, raw lump on the sand. Already they had shredded the clothing he wore in order to get at the goodies it concealed. As scavengers they were swift and efficient, but then most undisturbed ecologies have methods of cleaning up after something has died. Initially I had no doubt the body on the sand was that of Noone. I reckoned he had been forced into the rocks.

But there was too much wreckage spread along the base of the escarpment. Some fifty meters south of Noone's carcass, most of the stern half of a powder blue airfoil had come to rest. A few birds fluttered in the area, one or two coming to rest briefly before taking flight again as if startled. I slowed my craft and drew cautiously upon the wreckage, coasting in a semicircle to get a thorough view of the interior.

Frazier lay against the foot of the aft bench. His right hand was open and empty; the left rested limp on his chest, the forearm bent unnaturally and with both bones protruding. He had managed to tie a makeshift tourniquet around his upper left arm, but blood was still flowing, not leaking, from the burst flesh around the bones. Already a couple liters of it had formed a puddle on the deck. His right leg was bent at the knee at an unusual angle, and the way he seemed to be favoring his left side indicated possible broken ribs there. Small gouges in the bare skin of his arms and neck bespoke the impatience of the birds, and hinted strongly that he might be unable to move, possibly due to a broken back.

I perched a hip over the stern. The craft tottered slightly under my weight, but remained where it had lodged.   "Comfy?" I inquired.

An aggrieved expression briefly overwhelmed the agony in his eyes. Evidently he expected me to express some sympathy for him, or at least for his plight, on the basis of our earlier intimacies. Either the training regarding the relevance of bed events hadn't taken, or he'd never received it.

Droplets of blood flecked his lips, confirming internal injuries. "You're cruel," he gasped.

"I've received no orders to be cruel," I said. "What's Grenke up to?"

"Fuck you."

"Been there."

I glanced back toward the sand and the ocean. I recalled having seen some birds while on the beach before this assignment began, and perhaps a few small brown ones flitting here and there in Sayoun, but I had not realized until now just how many there were. Of course, most of the time they were probably perching in trees, taking shelter from the heat of the day.

"They seem to be very efficient scavengers," I said matter-of-factly. "Why, I'll bet they'll have that boy cleaned to the bones before long. They've already made short work of the clothing, it's in shreds. I wonder if he was still alive when the feasting started. Maybe they went for the eyes first. Eventually they found something vital--an artery, perhaps, or they tore at the heart while it was still beating." I paused, and looked him over. "It looks like you've managed to swat them away with one arm, so far. Maybe you'll last a while."

Frazier licked some of the blood from his lips. "You'd leave me here?"

"We're not known for our first aid skills."

"You're almost as cold as Grenke," he said.

"Colder. I'll designate perching positions for the smorgasbord. Grenke?"

It pained him to shake his head, but he managed. "Hasn't told us. The pay is good, but all we've had so far are orders."

"So why were you with the protest group?" I asked him.

"Infiltration. Find out what they were up to. Find a way to use them."

"Blame them for killings?"

He nodded once, and grimaced. "Then you showed up, and nobody knew who you were. Grenke thinks you're AmSec."

"What were your orders with regard to me?"

Again Frazier licked his lips, but did not respond.

"Let me guess," I said. "Keep an eye on me. Kill me if it could be done without attribution." I recalled that Frazier had appeared surprised at first when I had thrown the door open to him that night. "Such a simple matter for you to post the Scritchy surreptitiously as we were leaving my room for the little tour. Then Logrin kills Agate and tries to kill Diana and me out at the cove." I snapped my fingers, recalling something Kitch had told me about the man's name. "Oh, goddammit, Logrin! *Lohegrin*. The opera. Of course!"

Frazier stared up at me. "What?" he croaked.

"Never mind. Tell me this: why kill those three young men in Makalla?"

A weak frown crossed his lips. He seemed to be fading now, from blood loss. "What?"

"Three men from Ecotect, in a bungalow in Makalla," I said, puzzled.

His expression seemed sincere. "They were killed. You were seen heading south of there in an airfoil afterwards."

"I haven't killed anyone there," he protested.

I glanced out at the flock of birds. "What about Noone?"

Frazier had one last burst of strength left. "*He* ran into *me*!" he gasped, and fell limp, and closed his eyes. "He ran into me," he whispered. "He was panicked. No, the only person I was ordered to kill was you." He coughed, and added, "If it could be done safely."

"There's no such thing, in this business," I told him.

The implications of his protest were troublesome, for they suggested that other forces were also at work here, forces about which I knew nothing. The option of protecting Tillvan against everyone now rose to the fore. While I pondered that, a little sound from Frazier got my attention. His eyes were open once more, and he had turned his head slightly to see the birds on the sand.

"I have no right to ask . . . ," he said softly.

I brought the Stern to bear. "Everyone has *that* right," I told him, and fired a blue beam into his chest.

Afterwards, I headed back north, along the coastline, but slowly. I needed to evaluate the events of the day so far, but there were so many uncertainties now. Frazier's denial of the killings in Makalla had sounded credible. Perhaps he had participated in the beatings that had killed most of the former constables, and he had tried to kill me, but someone else, unknown to me and to Deven, had been busy in Makalla. And to what possible end? It made sense for Grenke to eliminate the Ecotect thorn in his side, and to eliminate the previous constables. It even made sense for him to have me killed or, failing that, to use me in indirect support of his operation, whatever it was. If not Grenke's long arm in Makalla, then whose? And why? And what did it have to do with my assignment?

The thought occurred that I needed a place and some time to think, to throw possibilities against a wall and see which ones stuck. Already I had reached the cove. Given its recent history, it was hardly a safe place for meditation, but I slowed the airfoil to hover just over the wet sand and looked around. I had seen the cove from above, from the crest of the escarpment. Now I had a view of it from the ocean. It looked like a cove. Something here commanded the interest of Amphictyony

Resources Corporation, and it warranted Grenke's activities, and I did not believe for a second that the two were compatible. All I could think of at the moment was beachfront property, but that might be developed without the efforts of AmResCor or Grenke. I had to find a new approach to the problem.

In that moment, I knew exactly what I needed. I peered up and down the beach and along the escarpment for Silver LeMay, but I did not spot her. Still, I had no doubt she was somewhere in the area, watching me. After docking down on the sand, I dug the bush hat from my pocket and waved it in a sweeping arc, back and forth.

Presently an airfoil appeared at the crest. A tallish woman with long, pale yellow hair stood on the bridge. For several seconds she gazed down at me, her expression unfathomable. She eased the airfoil to the left, where the escarpment had long ago given way, and deftly maneuvered her down over the rocks and rubble. After she reached the sand, her gaze did not waver from me during her approach. I stepped down onto the beach while she settled her airfoil, and waited.

LeMay's attire seemed unsuited to surveillance. A bandeau of apricot terrycloth secured above and below with elastic bands served as a top, leaving most of her upper body bare and with incipient sunburn. Black denim cutoffs and black hiking boots completed her outfit. The butt of the Ecko protruded from under her belt, a reminder of her deadly skills. The tentative smile on her lips matched the expression in her dove-gray eyes. She drew up within arm's reach and stood very still, leaving it to me to break the remainder of the impasse.

Several things I might say, some awkward and some profound, whisked through my thoughts without pause. Several options for physical response opened to me, including a few that were violent. Her expression told me nothing, nor did it betray any expectation. She stood willing to accept whatever response I might make.

In that moment I surrendered to myself. The assignment, Blacklight, the training, and my past all drifted away like dust in the wake of an airfoil, leaving behind an empty space that could best be filled by impulse. In that moment there was something I needed, more than anything else. I slipped my arms around Silver LeMay, drew her the last few centimeters to me, and held onto her for dear life.

Time counted, the way it does, while we stood there on the beach, her face pressed into my neck, mine into hers. There was too much to think about, so I thought nothing. There was too much to say, so I said nothing. Contentment filled the silence that enveloped us.

We were standing so motionless that, in a mad and incongruous moment, I began to worry that the birds might suppose us dead and edible. Silver leaned back to look at me, mirth making her eyes glow.

"What was that chuckle for?" she asked. I glanced at a couple birds perched nearby on the sand, and she said, "Oh."

"I know some moves that might scare them off," I told her.

Her smile hinted at mischief. "It's too sandy here. I have a place near Makalla," she added, stepping back from me. "A bungalow with a view of the ocean. Want to race?"

"Sure," I said, but she had already scrambled aboard her airfoil.

LeMay reached the bungalow first, because she knew its location-- about a kilometer south of Makalla--and because I still felt it prudent to keep her in front of me. With our physical separation my desire to act on impulse had diminished, and training and experience reasserted themselves. I had time, while pretending to race her, to consider the potential threat she represented to my assignment.

It seemed unlikely that LeMay was aware of the killings in Makalla. Even had she followed Kitch and me north, she would not have had time to investigate the bungalow before I turned back south. But I could not yet completely dismiss her as a suspect. She would know how to present herself as unaware. She surely was able to pass off the artificial as genuine.

The bungalow at which we had arrived was real enough. It stood alone among a cluster of curving, long-trunked trees at the edge of the beach, some hundred meters from the ocean's edge. Although it appeared to have been designed by the same architect as the other dwellings in the settlement, hers boasted a full covered patio facing the water, with a sloping overhang to ward off the occasional rains. A waist-high wall of white stone cordoned off the quarter-hectare of land occupied by the bungalow, and in the yard thus described stood a pair of trees whose tropical fruit was just beginning to turn blue. LeMay stood beneath one of them, in the shade, waiting for me to disembark.

I still did not trust her, but trust or the lack thereof had ceased to be an issue between us. Had LeMay been contracted to prevent me from completing my assignment, she would already have attempted to kill me.

While a good measure of paranoia is healthy in our line of work, at some point the walls have to be lowered, if for no other reason than to catch one's breath. I chose to proceed on the probability that Silver LeMay had no professional interest in my assignment. Insofar as I did not myself jeopardize it, I was free to indulge in those activities following which I would still have to catch my breath.

LeMay made a desultory gesture toward the patio, inviting me to a white wicker chair at the solitary round patio table. Evidently she was not yet ready to yield to her innuendoes--nor was I, despite a certain edginess that had come over me and that badly needed burring. After I sat down, LeMay swept inside and emerged presently with two dark brown glass bottles of *Weihenstephaner*, the caps already popped. These she placed carefully on the table top.

"There's one more thing to do," said LeMay, as she edged back toward the low wooden fence that surrounded the patio. "Take out your Stern and aim it at me."

I stiffened. "What?"

"Please."

Reluctantly I did so.

"I'm going to draw my sidearm," she announced, and after I nodded, did so, using only her thumb and index finger like a pincers. Very deliberately she deposited the weapon on the patio at the base of the fence, then returned to the table and sat down across from me, elbows aprop the table, chin resting on her hands.

"That was melodramatic and unnecessary," I said, and tucked the Stern back under my belt.

"And unconvincing. I understand." For just a moment her eyes darkened with sadness. She leaned forward, and spoke with an earnestness I did not doubt, because it shone through even though she had to believe I would doubt it. "Nyx . . . it's not that you don't trust me. It's that you are not capable of trust. I'm not sure I am, either. You've been too long doing what you do; so have I. But we don't have to trust each other to work together, whether on your assignment or on," she flicked her eyes toward the bungalow, "my bed."

"So you think you'd be safe from me in bed, unarmed."

A tiny smile toyed with the corners of her mouth while she sketched little slow circles in the condensation on the table with her beer bottle. "Your extra height would give you more leverage. I think maybe you're a little quicker. I might be more wiry. Unarmed combat would be interesting. We'd have to forego all killing maneuvers, and anything that would result in keeping us out of action for more than, say, a fortnight. But I'd love to go a few falls with you."

I stifled a laugh by biting my lower lip.

"Okay, that didn't come out the way I meant it," said LeMay. "Besides, that's not what you need right now."

"Try me."

LeMay shook her head. "This--you and I sitting here, on this patio with a couple of beers--this is what you need right now. I know this, because back there on the beach, you didn't kiss me. You held me. Adhered to me, really."

"Who else can I talk shop with, you mean?"

"Exactly!" She grinned, then sobered, and seemed to reach a decision. "But it's more than that. Nyx . . . I was hired by Ecotect to protect you."

For just a moment, my heart felt as if it had spilled off a ledge. Of its own volition, my hand twitched toward the Krupp Stern. "You were doing just fine until now," I said glumly. "There's no way Ecotect could have known I would be assigned here."

LeMay made a face. "Again I misspoke. I was hired to protect whomever was assigned. That turned out to be you." She held out her bottle, and we tapped necks together and took gulps. "I'm glad it was."

"I still have problems," I said. "Given what you've told me, Ecotect knew in advance that a situation would develop here that would require the intervention of someone . . . like me."

"Of Blacklight, yes." LeMay drained a third of her bottle. "It wasn't difficult to work out. Ecotect keeps track of AmResCor plans and probes. About a year ago a probe turned up evidence of a huge deposit of niobium here in the area around that cove."

"Those black streaks," I said, "in the granite?"

"Much more just under the surface. Seismic analyses suggest the deposit is extensive and readily accessible. The cove itself would be destroyed by the extraction process, of course. AmResCor cut orders that were to dispatch Manager Terreme to check out the site physically, without drawing attention to himself. Someone got wind of those orders, and hired a team to discourage AmResCor and to secure the deposit for himself."

"Who? Not Grenke, surely."

"Grenke is just a highly skilled mirror-fogger. Someone hired him. I don't know who. I wasn't told. I don't think Ecotect knows. But the point here is that the threat to Amphictyony Resources Corporation became known. AmResCor Security was deemed ineffectual in this situation, because it is geared less toward removals and more toward enforcement and prosecution, which seldom is proof against assassination. So the corporation turned to Blacklight--too late, as it happened, because initially you were to be ordered to protect Terreme."

"None of this was in my briefing," I told her. "Deven omits things on occasion, but he always gives me all the information I need to fulfill the assignment."

"He probably wasn't told everything."

"He did suggest that someone might try to be clever," I admitted. "That's why he ordered your removal. He wanted to find out who would complain."

"Finish your beer."

"Almost there. Diana, last night---"

"You shoved me away," she interrupted gently. "You had to. I understand. But now I hope something has changed in your orders."

"That's an odd thing to say."

Pale yellow hair swirled as she shook her head. "Not at all. Much of the attraction you hold for me is that you are who you are, Nyx. If you have changed, even if for my benefit, then you are becoming less than who you are. I would not want that."

"Even if it meant your life?"

She shrugged. "I'll take my chances. I always have."

"I suggested to Deven that if someone wants you dead, it might be to our advantage to keep you alive," I told her. "He concurred with that reasoning."

She cocked an eyebrow at me. "Someone? Meaning AmResCor?"

"Well, they originated the tasking." I sat back and savored the last of the beer. "So. Why does Ecotect want me safe?"

"Ecotect is going to be blamed for Terreme's killing, and that of his replacement, and probably for the loss of the deposit if someone else takes it over," explained LeMay. "It will be difficult, but Ecotect can deal with that. As I said earlier, security's weapons are procedural: enforcement and prosecution. But Blacklight has its own rules. Ecotect does not want you folks coming after it in retaliation, should you be killed. And it would be held responsible for that, because all the evidence has been arranged to point in its direction. Blacklight is not known for asking questions. Ecotect is well aware of this. Thus my contract." She got to her feet. "Another beer?"

"Maybe afterwards."

She shot me an arch look. "Afterwards, is it?"

"I meant that now I ought to bring you up to date."

"Well of course you did. What *was* I thinking?"

"Silver---"

"Uh-uh. We're not in bed yet."

". . . I don't think we're going to make it to the bed."

We didn't.

010

From dozing I drifted awake, to find myself in a tangle of arms and legs, on a futon in the front room we had managed to stagger and crawl to. Beside me stirred Silver LeMay, sensitive to the change in my respiration. Her eyelashes tickled the side of my neck.

There was nothing to say. After we had exhausted ourselves, we had drifted off while engaged in those little murmurings that flow from jumbled thoughts and sated desires. Most of the sounds were incomprehensible, and we understood them only through our exposed vulnerabilities. Given the realities of our work and the dictum regarding what happens in bed, I was unable to consider what we had done as acts of love. Nevertheless, I felt something, and I felt it strongly enough that I did not need to formally express it.

"Another beer?" whispered Silver.

"Not without eating something first."

"Um . . . I'm not touching that line."

I eased my face away, and saw my reflection in eyes of soft silver gray above mine. "Don't tell me you're still on."

Very delicately, Silver shifted position, her ruff catching lightly on mine, an unspoken tease. "Well . . . I haven't indulged in my personal kink yet."

"Let's save the bush hat for a special occasion," I suggested.

She ducked her face against the outer swell of my right breast and nuzzled the tattoo there. "What does this mean: All But Nine?"

"From another time and place, Silver," I replied. "It represented an attitude, me against the Universe. Long long ago it was an aphorism among battle-weary soldiers. 'Fuck 'em all but nine: six to carry the casket, two for road guards, and one to count cadence.'"

She lifted her head, and our eyes met again. "Maybe . . . maybe someday, 'All But Ten?'"

The question brought a memory out of its dark nook, and for just a moment my eyes filmed over. I blinked them clear. My voice was stronger than I thought it would be. "I don't want to alter the tattoo," I said, as I had once said to another, similar request. "You can be a road guard."

"That's well within the purview of my present contract." She sat up, momentarily astride me, then stood and began to gather our discarded clothing. Ruefully she held up my top for inspection. Both spaghetti straps had snapped during the process of disrobing. She cast the garment aside. "I'm sure I have something here that you can wear," she told me, tossing my denims onto the futon, the Stern inside them. Pausing, she gave me a sidelong look. "Would you like to shower first?"

"Together?"

"Well . . . I do have a fresh bar of cinnamon-scented glycerin soap."

Eventually, refreshed and bedraggled, we emerged from the stall. The skin on my extremities was wrinkled, a tribute to the duration of our ablutions. LeMay's bungalow held a supply of hot water sufficient to allow a long, lingering lathering, followed by . . . well, you can cut a few more meters of cloth from that bolt and make of it what you want. Already the day had reached the mid-afternoon, and I had yet to set an agenda. Deven had issued a simple instruction--protect Tillvan--and left up to me the method by which I would accomplish that. As yet I felt no sense of urgency, but Silver LeMay, naked, continued to provide a distraction, and I had to force myself to dress.

Seeing what I was about, LeMay said, "There are fresh underpads in the nightstand drawer."

I found on and affixed it, then grabbed my denims from the futon and stepped into them. "You came prepared for a possible guest," I observed.

"Not . . . exactly," said Silver. "I live here, now and then. This is my *pied à terre*, one of them. That's why I've been careful about Diana. Here on Adenne I'm Diana Silberstein. Shower again tonight, perhaps?"

I glanced up from fastening my boots. "I'm staying here?"

Silver entered her bedroom, and peered back around the door jamb. "Please?"

"Well, I can't go back to Sayoun right now," I called, while she rummaged around for attire. Presently she emerged, dressed in white shorts and a pullover one shade darker than her hair, and tossed a black cotton bandeau at me. "I didn't leave much there in the *Pestle*," I added, adjusting the top around me. "Just a change of clothes and some toiletries."

"I have spares," said Silver, and sat down on the futon. I caught a whiff of cinnamon, which I supposed was an after-effect of the soap. Its source, however, was a small vial that she passed to me.

"Unless you want to remote your 'skip here and resupply," she added, while I dabbed myself here and there.

"That might attract attention."

She tugged at my hand until I dropped down beside her. "Then it's time you brought me up to date," she said.

*　　　*　　　*

In the event, I disclosed all my mission-related information to Silver LeMay. To assist me properly, she needed to know what I knew and what I had already surmised. But there was one other matter to attend to, and she stunned me with its simple clarity.

"Do you have a fiver?" LeMay asked, when I had finished my briefing.

Scowling, I dug out my fundsclip, peeled off a green and gold AV5 certificate, the lowest denomination issued, and pressed it into her outstretched palm.

She folded the note in half, slipped it into her pocket, and smiled brightly. "So let's get to work," she said.

"Goddamn mercenary," I muttered. But I said it fondly, and not without some relief. Having now contracted LeMay for a short-term and specific purpose that dovetailed nicely with her own assignment, I could count on her as a pro to act in concert with me. The AV5 effectively lowered the last barrier between us, at least until my mission was completed.

LeMay got up and went out to the patio, returning with her Ecko, which she tucked under the waistband of her shorts. She paused briefly, regarding me, head tilted to one side and a crooked smile on her lips, and vanished into the dinette. I heard doors open and close, utensils clatter, and some other sounds not readily identifiable. Finally she returned to the front room bearing a small platter containing small chunks of pale yellow cheese and tureens filled with pickled olives or small bits of dried fruit. This she placed atop a small table which she pulled within easy reach of the futon, and sat down beside me.

"*Mangia, mangia,*" she invited.

I selected a cheese chunk. It was soft and a bit chewy, and without a strong flavor, and it reminded me that I had not yet even taken breakfast.

"The fundamental problem here is protecting Tillvan," said LeMay, between bites. "He'll probably refuse to go into seclusion or isolation, and we can't be certain of the placement of the opposition." She paused, and grinned wickedly. "The solution is obvious."

I tried a green olive stuffed with garlic. "Hide in plain sight."

LeMay pouted, but her eyes laughed. "You're no fun."

"Once you said it was obvious, I saw it. Very few people know what Tillvan looks like, plus we can commo ahead and have him alter his appearance. Once we have him in tow, we can get him made up, dye his hair, whatever needs to be done. Tillvan will become a tourist. The opposition knows me, so I'll have to lurk. You'll have to be his escort. He'll want to take you places, right? So he can go on his precious exploratory excursions, and no one will be the wiser."

LeMay looked thoughtful. "They know he's going to arrive tomorrow night. As soon as they've identified him, he's done." She paused, and glanced at me. "Do you really think there's another rifle out there?"

"It makes sense," I said. "There's a missing box of ammo. There's not much cover around the Spaceport, but several of the buildings could provide a suitable firing point." I shrugged. "If it's me, I make the nock at the Spaceport. He'll be stationary there, or relatively so. En route to Sayoun, he's a moving target, more difficult to hit with a bullet."

"But not with an ergorifle," LeMay pointed out.

"Maybe," I conceded, "if they miss the opportunity at the Spaceport. They might station a backup sniper along the glideway to wait for the public conveyance. But Tillvan would still be a moving target, and seated among other passengers. Very difficult shot."

"Not one I would want to try," agreed LeMay.

"But if Tillvan has let an airfoil," I said, thinking aloud, "to be waiting for him upon his arrival."

"Easy enough to check," said LeMay. "Emmix Transport is the only place to let an airfoil in this region of Equatoria. They'll have records. They might not have Tillvan's name on them, but all we need to know is whether there will be an airfoil awaiting pickup at the Spaceport."

I stretched my legs and gazed out at my boots, and grimaced. "There's one other matter."

"Kitch," said LeMay. "A ruse. A bit of misdirection."

I made a little sound of disgust. "I don't know why I don't just let you plan this entire operation."

"Hey, you did hire me, you know."

I dug out the PHL and had Niobe raise the fire station.

There was no response.

011

By the time we reached the fire station I had briefed LeMay on what I knew of its interior layout. We made a complete circle around the building, then rose to check the roof, but saw no other conveyances. I docked down by the great fruit tree and we swept toward the side door, weapons out, in the one-by formation Blacklight teaches, LeMay covering the left side and rear. The side door was ajar, and allowed LeMay the best view of the immediate interior hallway to our right. I nudged the door open, and with her covering me, rolled inside and to the left.

The hallway was empty. All three doors were open. I pushed the side door until it abutted the wall, then waggled my Stern at the treatment room. While LeMay went to check it out, I peered cautiously into the second room, and learned that it was unoccupied--evidently it was intended for equipment storage.

Without much enthusiasm I moved on to the third doorway,

Rigantonio's office. Already I had caught a whiff of feces, a body having evacuated itself after death, and knew what I would find. Rigantonio was sitting in his office chair, leaning back, head thrown back, staring up at the ceiling. His left arm perched precariously on the armrest, his right dangled over the side. A discoloration on his left cheekbone and a bloody patch behind his left ear suggested the cause of death. Probably he had died upon receiving those two blows, depriving Grenke of his little pleasures.

I gave the room a cursory search. Although awash with clutter, Rigantonio's desk showed no signs of having been searched. The few bits of furniture matched what I recalled from my first visit. To the casual observer, it appeared that Rigantonio might have fallen, injuring himself, had sat down to recover, and died in his chair. Obviously the scene had been set that way. It made sense if Grenke was covering his tracks. With Rigantonio dead by misadventure, nobody would bother looking for a broader crime scene.

A door in the rear of the office gave onto the open bay, where a pair of airfoils were docked, one for paramedic use, the other to transport water and fire-retardants to small fires. After verifying that the bay and conveyances were unoccupied, I returned to the office.

"Nyx?" called LeMay.

"Be there in a sec."

I set my hand over Rigantonio's eyes and slid the eyelids closed. Rigor mortis had worn off, and his hands and wrists showed signs of blood settling. I leaned him forward, so that his head rested on crossed forearms, and left him to dream forever of a young woman on his arm.

LeMay was waiting for me by the doorway, Ecko in her right hand, lowered by her side. "Rigantonio's dead," I told her. "Find anything?"

"Drops and smears of blood, consistent with an injured person undergoing treatment while seated in a chair," she said. "No sign of a struggle. No sign of Kitch." She paused, and frowned. "So they took the others and left Rigantonio here. Setting a scene?"

"That's what I figure. Grenke didn't count on Hokins surviving his attentions. I'm guessing he originally had planned to dispose of the bodies, perhaps at the crematorium, but Hokins' escape spoiled that idea. Grenke had no idea where they went. It was a loose end. Not a critical one, to be sure. But something keyed him."

"In point of fact, it's Hawkins," said LeMay.

I docked on a metal examining table, and continued. "Let's figure either Rigantonio or Kitch made contact with the crematorium in Sayoun. When the crematorium learned that the three bodies in the bungalow were murder victims, it followed standard operating procedure and alerted the Constabulary. That's all Grenke needed. He would assume the bodies were those of the missing constables. The crematorium informed him of who reported the bodies, and he and perhaps one or two others proceeded to the fire station, briefly interrogated Rigantonio and learned that the other bodies had already been buried, killed Hawkins and disposed of his body--the ocean is a good place for that."

"And Kitch?" prompted LeMay.

"Yes. Kitch."

After a short silence, LeMay asked, "Would Grenke have known who Kitch really was?"

"If he did, she's alive," I said evenly. "If he didn't, she's in the ocean with Hawkins."

"Agreed." She gave me a sidelong glance. "We could try to rescue her."

"We're not in the business of rescuing damsels in distress," I replied.

"That's the generic response," said LeMay, nodding.

"Still . . . she would be useful in identifying her father for us when he arrives tomorrow evening. If we had an idea of where to look for her. You know the topography better than I do."

LeMay gazed at me speculatively. "Nice temporizing," she said softly. Then, louder: "Grenke quarters in the Constabulary. The associate constables are dispersed among various inns. Even if we could take them all out, we still don't know who's issuing the orders." She made a little gesture with the Ecko. "Let's get out of here," she recommended, and I followed her out the door.

*   *   *

I reckoned we would head back to LeMay's bungalow or perhaps further, to the seacoast, but instead she directed me toward the interior. As I've indicated, the western coastline of the southern half of Equatoria angles slightly to the east, and the terrain is mostly scrub and semi-desert, with large oases here and there, such as in the area of Sayoun, and Makalla to the north. Shiere, a coastal village farther south, lies close to the temperate zone. A range of weathered foothills parallels the coastline about fifty kilometers to the east, and beyond that, according to the topographical holograms afforded me by Niobe, my 'skipcomp, spreads forest and savannah nurtured by seasonal rains. As far as I was aware, that area held no mission interest for me, and LeMay was not forthcoming with regard to her intentions.

Of necessity LeMay kept watch aft. She stood against the console, legs braced, hair whipping around her, arms folded across her chest. After boarding up and pointing me in the direction she wanted to go, she had uttered not a word, and her expression was difficult to read. Pensive, perhaps, with a dash of concern. From time to time I threw a glance over my shoulder, wondering whether someone had offered pursuit and thereby had wrinkled her brow, but I saw nothing to be alarmed about.

Finally she said, in a voice just loud enough to be heard over the breeze, "I'd tell you if there were someone behind us."

"Was it something I said?"

"Yes."

I decided not to pursue the matter. For one thing, we were coming up on a patch of rugged terrain where, long ago, torrential rains had eroded gullies and washes. Most of them seemed to lead toward the southwest, possibly to an ancient riverbed. The irregular surface mandated manual control, and I switched off the groundhug app and took us up another meter to avoid the boulders and flora that relieved the otherwise empty terrain. Already grays had begun to replace the blues in the eastern horizon. Night fell quickly here, and I wondered how much further we had to travel.

"Just over that rise," said LeMay, without looking ahead. "About another ten kilometers."

I had no need to ask how she had known what to tell me. She was a pro; had our positions been reversed, she would have wondered where we were headed, as I had. But the faux telepathy reminded me of a story I'd read, sneaking into the school library at night, wherein Poe's detective Dupin was able to construct entire swatches of dialogue based on his observations of body language, mannerisms, and expressions. For just a moment I felt like a psychological sidekick.

"I almost quit, once," said LeMay, gazing back toward the seacoast, now lost in the horizon. For several seconds she added nothing to this revelation, nor did I feel it incumbent upon me to encourage her. Who else can I talk shop with? might be a rationale, but I had not sensed any flagging of purpose in myself, and certainly felt no urge to discuss the possibility of it. But LeMay did not see that in me.

"It was early years," she went on at last. She drew in a slight breath, as if she had just caught a thorn under her fingernail. "I really had not given much thought as to what I could or could not be paid to do. I hadn't realized, until the opportunity presented itself, that there were some things--at least one thing--I was not willing to do."

In the pause that followed, I said, "Is this something I really need to know, Silver?"

"Bring the craft to hover, please," she replied, and I did so. The eastern horizon had darkened now, and night was sweeping the light from the land. We had perhaps half an hour before dark.

"I was asked to kill a child," she said, just above a whisper. "I had already agreed to a contract to kill the father. His wife and daughter were add-ons. I . . . "

She fell silent to give me an opportunity to encourage her, to tell her to continue, and I could not do it. She had entered a psychological and emotional area that did not belong to me. She seemed to be suggesting that I might be willing under certain circumstances to refuse an order from Deven, and of course I would do no such thing. But she seemed also to have some purpose in this revelation. I waited.

"I fulfilled only the first part of the contract," LeMay continued, with an uncertain glance in my direction, as if I had disappointed her in some way. "Later, another mortifice completed what I had left undone. For a brief time afterwards I doubted myself. I won't trouble you with the inner conflict, but when I had resolved it, I found that I could have scruples and still be very, very good at my work. These did not diminish me in any way. This is a cold occupation." Her brow knit for a moment, and then she shook her head. "No, this occupation *requires* a coldness of heart, a clinical, almost mechanical process. It is up to me to set my standards." Through clenched jaws she added, "There are in fact some things I won't do."

"And you are telling me this because?"

LeMay give a little nod of approval. "Very cold," she said. "Very good. That continues undiminished in you, as it should. It makes you you."

"I sense a 'but' coming on," I said, almost against my will. I mean, the last thing I wanted to do was give her a reason to go on in this vein.

"Would you carry out an order to kill a friend, a lover?" she asked.

"Sure."

But I had answered too quickly. It was the proper response, to be sure, derived from training and hard experience, but even in my own ears it sounded flippant, as if I had not meant it. In the back of my mind a question reared its ugly head: what if I didn't mean it? Deven's face, hovering over my mind like a moon, nodded approval as I stomped the question back into oblivion.

In the incipient dusk, still leaning against the console, LeMay slowly turned her head and looked directly at me. Her eyes glistened like chips of cracked diamond. The corners of her mouth trembled in an almost-smile. I knew where she was going with this line of thinking, of course, and I found it difficult to believe that she would even hint that I might ignore or circumvent the rule about what happens in bed. She was a pro, damn it. She was *supposed* to be a pro.

"Yet you didn't carry out such an order while we were, at best, acquaintances," she whispered.

The words abraded me. I knew what I was doing--I was aware of what I was doing--when I had denied her and sent her away the night before, but I had not fully acknowledged to myself what I was doing. I *had*, in effect, refused an order from Deven. For just an instant there was a stranger in my mirror. Then the image became me again, and I could not tell the difference.

"I don't love you," I said.

"I don't love you, either."

"Well, there we are, then."

"Here we are, then," she amended, and sighed. "Well, at least you trust me."

"Don't kid yourself . . . "

"Silver," she supplied, for the space I had left. "Diana, on Adenne, when we're not alone."

"We're not in bed."

She shrugged lightly. "Easily remedied. And yes, you *do* trust me."

"Silver---"

"Why are you here?" she snapped. I gave her a blank look, and she said, "After we left the fire station, all I did was tell you to bear east, and you did. No questions, no objections, nothing. You powered up and took us east. You *trusted* me. You took me on faith, if you will. And now

106

here we are."

"You set me up," I said, scowling. "There's nothing out here."

"That's right."

"This whole trip was just to prove a point."

"Pretty much," she agreed.

She refrained from pointing out that my recognition of her purpose implied that she had indeed proved her point. However, we remained on the same wavelength, and I was all too aware of that implication. For just an instant I felt caged, and the only way to unlock the door was to demonstrate that she was wrong, wrong. All the while LeMay's arms remained folded while she studied me, a live bug she had pinned to the display box. My right hand twitched. She might have skewered me with logic, but a blue beam from the Stern could liberate me.

LeMay merely looked at me, and did not tell me that she was right. Instead, she said, quietly, "Acceptance did not come immediately for me, Nyx. It may take a while for you, too. Sometimes I wonder whether there is an eternal truth that underlies one's choices, whether each of us has one thing--at least one thing--that regardless of conditions or pressures we will not do. Maybe there's some universal statement inherent in each of us, that we rarely even give voice to, but we recognize it when the opportunity arises. No, I will not do that. Nyx? Nyx!"

"What?" I hissed, my hand still a bundle of poised nerves.

"Kill you. Harm you. Betray you. I will not do that."

I made a fist of my right hand for control, and gave a little nod. Training was especially unhelpful in these circumstances, because it had wiped away whatever I might have thought. Was supposed to have wiped it away. Yet here I stood, having disobeyed Deven's original orders regarding LeMay, or at best having dodged them, and having taken a journey of misdirection solely at the behest of a woman who just yesterday I was supposed to have killed. Reality trumps rationales. I had come to the cusp of an understanding.

"Deven is not going to like this," I said.

"Is it necessary to tell him?"

I looked back toward the eastern horizon. "You said ten more kilometers. What's there?"

"An oasis." She turned back around, hands resting lightly on the console, her purpose for the moment fulfilled. "Best to avoid the place at night. All manner of creatures will be drinking there, now that the air has cooled. Some of them will be predators, a few of them even large enough to give us a bad moment or two if we were on the ground. Are you hungry?"

"I suppose we could proceed to your oasis and find something to kill, dress out, and roast."

"Or dine on something at my bungalow," said LeMay, and that set our destination for the evening.

I turned off the bowlamp for security before we reached Makalla, and after a pause to get my night vision, navigated around to the south of the settlement and thence to the coast. Luminescent wave crests added almost as much light as the chips of crystal in the night canopy. Out over the waves a bird cried, and as I searched for it I realized that no stars shone to the south and west. The wind had changed, too, coming up from the south now, with gusts strong enough to torment the loose white beach sand, and I had to steady the helm in the cross-current before banking north toward LeMay's bungalow.

"The season starts early this year," said LeMay.

"How bad will this one get?" I asked her.

"There's no lightning yet. Maybe it will be a mild one."

LeMay dug out her PHL and called up the local meteorological display from one of the METSATs, projecting it onto the console. The ocean appeared in blue, the land brown, and a vast, swirling mass of various shades of gray appeared over the rear, or southern, portion of the holographic display. A flash of white lit up the gray mass, and even in that same instant a brief glow from the rear enveloped us.

The wind picked up, whipping LeMay's hair across her eyes, and she gathered it in one hand and held it in place on her shoulder. With the thumb and middle finger of her other hand she compassed distance, and said, "It will hit Makalla in about half an hour. It's not as bad as it looks, I've been through several of them. But if you wouldn't mind accelerating . . .?"

I did so. Wind from our rear and from port buffeted us, but I managed to hold course. After LeMay disabled the projection, she studied the shoreline for her waypoints, and finally directed me further ashore. I caught a glimpse of her bungalow silhouetted against a few lights that shone about a kilometer to the northwest, where spread the main portion of the settlement. Already some of the spindly coastal trees were bent like longbows, and I could hear the wind sifting through the fronds. LeMay keyed her PHL once more, and directed me to the east side of the bungalow, where the door now stood open to a bay of mortared stone walls. I docked beside her airfoil, she closed the door behind us, and we disembarked.

After she checked her failsafes and we searched the bungalow, LeMay immediately made for the patio, and began dragging the wicker furniture inside. I retrieved an overturned chair, and collected a potted plant. Within a couple minutes we had rescued everything that might have blown away. Gusts of wind laden with sea foam hissed at us, and struck the patio windows.

Secure inside the front room, I peered out into the night and the storm, though the patio overhang blocked most of my view. My right side felt warm; LeMay had drawn up beside me.

"The patio and the bungalow are titanium frame set in concrete," she told me. "The roof can withstand steady winds of 250 kph. The two fruit trees have deep taproots." Sand ticked the windows, and her hand came to rest on my shoulder. "Power for the bungalow is self-contained," she added. "We won't lose it. So," she finished, stepping around to face me, "how would you like to ride out this storm?"

An impulse to frivolity shook me. I wanted to laugh. I wanted to lean slightly forward and kiss LeMay on the tip of her nose. I wanted to grab hold of her and never let go, and worst of all, for just an instant I wanted nothing more to do with Blacklight. But the moment passed, replaced by a tingly wave of heat that began in my legs and wound up on my face, and I was aware of LeMay gazing at me curiously.

"You're flushed," she observed. "I can't believe the question embarrassed you."

"I just had a mad moment."

She took my hand and tugged me toward the kitchen. "Do you have many of those?"

"Not that I usually indulge in."

"Ah, indulge. What a delightful verb." We reached the kitchen, and she opened the cooler. "I can offer you French bread, goat cheese, pickled olives, and smoked ham," she announced. "I assume you'll trust me with the bread knife?"

A peal of thunder shook the bungalow, and the lights flickered momentarily. All my training and instincts took over. I snatched the Stern, but LeMay had already closed on me, one arm encircling me, and I was unable to bring the weapon to bear. I tried a couple moves, and learned that she had read the same book. At my ear her lips moved like fluttering flower petals. "It's all right," she whispered. "That happens sometimes."

Air left me. I felt as if I had missed something I didn't know I was supposed to have had. I set the Stern on the counter beside me, and LeMay released my wrist and eased back a pace. A trace of amusement blended with the question in her pale eyes.

I knew what she would ask, of course. I had responded to the unexpected threat of darkness in the presence of a potential adversary as I had been trained to do. LeMay's defensive encirclement had been skillful, but not without counters. How hard had I tried to extricate myself? Any one of three or four relatively simple maneuvers should have sufficed. She had approached me with one thought in mind: to reassure me against the storm. She had done that, knowing that I would react according to training. The abrupt rush toward me had placed her in far worse jeopardy than the flickering of the lights, and she had to have known that as well. And yet . . .

I swore softly.

LeMay gave me a sidelong glance. "What?"

"Silver, I really don't know."

"Then perhaps we should retreat to the olives and the cheese."

The storm passed without much effect. A comb of seaweed draped itself over the balustrade, and a seabird, caught in a gust, caromed off the patio roof. Soon enough the tall trees straightened, the dark canopy cleared, and the bottle of Sancerre stood empty on an end table beside a platter with a few crusts of bread. My head swam a bit, from the wine and from the immersion into unfamiliar territory.

By this time I had no doubt whatsoever that Silver LeMay had meant every word she had uttered with regard to our relationship and her emotions associated with it. The earnestness was a bit disconcerting. My mind castigated her as unprofessional, yet I knew the charge was unfounded. But what was the source of that knowledge? Were I considering opposites, I should have said that it came from my heart. But I had no heart, not of the sort she was seeking. During a solitary childhood I'd never developed one, and anything that might have arisen later had died stillborn at the hands of my Blacklight trainers.

Or had it? I discovered that whenever I looked at LeMay, I felt what I could only describe as a kinship. *Who else can I talk shop with?* But was that kinship something that I would not be willing to destroy, even if so ordered? I looked at her, and I could not answer. Perhaps that, in itself, was an answer.

While I was pondering this, LeMay broke a quarter hour of silence.

"We have perhaps eight hours until sunrise," she said.

I nodded. My head swam even more.

"We can finalize our plans in the morning," she said.

"One of those words sounded like 'bedroom.'"

This time we made it that far.

012

Bright daylight intruded upon us. We awoke almost simultaneously to the realization that we had no more time to laze about under the warm quilt. After a stretch or two to untangle the kinks and tendons, we raced each other to her hygiene alcove. We took turns, in the shower and out, and dried each other with exaggerated chasteness, laughing all the while. Temptation lingered, but only for a moment. Again the nature of the day before us snagged our thoughts.

LeMay found some attire that fit me reasonably well--black denims and a green camouflage pullover, if it matters--and selected for herself a similar outfit, the top done in desert tans. Finally we repaired to the futon with a couple of baguettes and a tub of real butter, and sat dangling our legs over the side, munching.

After we had devoured one of the baguettes, LeMay drew a deep breath and let it out slowly, then turned to me, shoulders squared, anticipation darkening her eyes to slate.

Ticking off the points on mental fingers, I said, "We need to reconnoiter the Spaceport, to determine the best place to grab Tillvan and get him quickly out of sight. We also need to check the records at Emmix Transport for airfoils to be left waiting out there. It would be nice to know the disposition and exact number of Grenke's people."

"And to reduce that number?" LeMay put in.

I thought about that. "This is the critical day for Grenke," I said. "He has his own operation, certainly already planned. I'm indirectly responsible for the loss of three of his people. My guess is that they'll be secluded until it's time to move. It will take time for us to find them. Even if we do manage to locate one or two of them and pick them off, Grenke will send the rest further into hiding."

"Unless they're already in place," LeMay pointed out.

"We'll watch for them at the Spaceport, of course," I said. "But the most difficult phase of hunting is the wait in the blind for the prey to show. Grenke is probably capable of it. But I doubt his minions will show much patience, and he'll have already taken that into account. He won't keep them waiting. I would like us to be in place before they do arrive, though."

"There's a row of kiosks next to the terminal itself that can provide us with social cover." She mulled this over, and gave a little nod. "After we have Tillvan, what do you want to do with him?"

Suddenly I swore, using plenty of hyphens. LeMay, taken aback by the outburst, stared at me with wide eyes. "It's this goddamn assignment," I explained. "I'm just not accustomed to keeping people alive."

"I can imagine," LeMay said. Grinning after my outburst, she deliberately picked up the two butter knives and set them out of my reach.

I bit my lip to stifle a laugh. "Pick him up and bring him here. I'll lay by at the Spaceport and cover you. Simple."

LeMay mulled this over for a few seconds, and nodded slowly. "It will be dark, or close to it," she said. "I can glide with the bowlamp off. They shouldn't acquire me." She paused, and added, "He'll have questions, you know, once he realizes we're not headed for Sayoun."

"If he starts to get out of hand, subdue him, secure him, and if necessary, gag him. I'll explain matters to him after I catch you up."

"That's all right, then. I wanted to know how far I could go."

I dug out my PHL. "I have to commo headquarters," I told her.

"Want me to leave?"

"It might be prudent," I said. "Canceling the order against you went against his grain a bit. I don't want to rub his nose in it by having you here."

LeMay got to her feet. "I'll just wait in the," and she paused, and ran the tip of her tongue over her lips, "bedroom."

"I'm on duty," I told her. "I'm imperturbable."

"Ah! That explains the smoky voice."

I waited until she was out of sight, and raised Deven. As always, he responded immediately. There's a rumor circulating around Blacklight that he actually does sleep, but I've never caught him at it. He'll send us to our demise without a milliqualm, but whenever we need him, he's there. I had Niobe cast his hologram onto the floor about two meters from the futon, and configure the image to that of a leprechaun.

Deven was his usual terse self. "Yes, Lieutenant?"

"I might not be able to commo in four hours on schedule, sir."

"Indeed." His eyes shifted from side to side, taking in my surroundings, which Niobe was projecting into his office, on the floor in front of his desk. Presumably he did not need to reconfigure my hologram to prevent identification. "You do not appear to be in a stay-the-night."

"I had to seek other lodgings, sir," I said, and brought him up to date while minimizing LeMay's role. Behind me I heard what I could only describe as tittering. Apparently LeMay had peeked around the corner, or otherwise spotted Deven's reflection.

"Does something about your assignment amuse you, Lieutenant?" he asked, after I had finished.

"Sorry, sir," I said, casting a mental instruction at LeMay to stifle herself. "If it's available, I'd like an up-to-date hologram of Tillvan uploaded to Niobe. Apparently very few people know what he looks like, and the images in the dossier you sent me are old. Based on how he appeared three years ago, I'd like instructions transmitted to him, advising him to shorten his hair, darken his skin to that of, say, a surfer, and if he could somehow acquire facial hair, that would be of even more help. I don't want him in office wear or other formal attire; I want him to dress as a tourist of moderate means."

The leprechaun that was Deven nodded thoughtfully. "You've promoted a 'purloined letter' solution. Tillvan can then go about his business without appearing to do so. You'll have to keep on the move, of course, but that would fit with his purported status. Where do you intend to quarter?"

He was Deven, and while I agreed with LeMay that there might indeed be at least one thing that I absolutely would not do, outright lying to him was not one of them. Steeling myself for his reaction, I gave him the truth. "Silver LeMay has a bungalow on the coast just south of Makalla, sir. It's conveniently located for Tillvan's explorations, and has better security than any stay-the-night in Sayoun."

The leprechaun image frowned so hard that it began to resemble a troll. He seemed to be mulling over various responses. "I hope you know what you're doing, Lieutenant," he said at last. "I'll have those instructions forwarded, and you'll have that hologram within the hour. I gather you're going to have Niobe adjust his image to match the description you want."

"Yes, sir. Are there any updates on stolen rifles?"

"Nothing new has been reported to me as yet," said Deven. The leprechaun tilted its head slightly. "You look as if you want to add something, Lieutenant."

"Just a thought, sir. We know that at least two of Grenke's associate constables were armed with Kellogg-Feuers. It seems reasonable to suppose that the others are similarly armed." I gave him the serial number I'd memorized from Frazier's sidearm. "Let's find out where it came from."

"Very well. Report as close to schedule as possible, Lieutenant."

After the leprechaun faded, LeMay emerged from the bedroom, her brow wrinkled in thought. On the way to the futon she drew a flavored meat stick from a canister on an end table and bit off a chunk, offering me the stick as she sat down.

"Garlic," I noted, catching a strong whiff of it.

"Fire with fire?" offered LeMay.

I declined with a shake of my head, and she leaned forward, elbows aprop knees, hair dangling along her cheeks.

"Someone shot at you on the beach," she said quietly. "Someone shot and killed Associate Constable Munro in the doorway of the Constabulary. Both of those were rifle shots. Later, someone killed those three young men here in Makalla."

LeMay had something on her mind, and I thought it best not to interrupt her train of thought. She gave me a sidelong glance, and added, "You've already suggested an unknown factor at work here. Maybe there's two."

114

"Most of the pieces are missing from the puzzle," I told her. "I don't doubt the events are somehow associated with my assignment, but without more information, I can only keep them filed, pending."

"Not so, *p'tite*," she countered. "Whoever took that shot at you on the beach knew in advance that you were a worthwhile target. Moreover, there's every possibility that he deliberately missed you. He certainly took out Terreme with a single shot. Weren't you at approximately the same range?"

"*P'tite?*" I said. I did not quite laugh.

She shrugged. "French has the best endearments." She shot me a worried look, and added, "Unless you think it's too soon in the relationship."

"But . . . '*p'tite?*'"

She dropped a kiss on my shoulder. "So why would he deliberately miss, do you think?"

I thought back to the event. "It was a close miss," I said, realization dawning. "He wanted me to know he was firing at me."

"Mmm. Let's leave that for a moment. Go to the Constabulary. You suspected he was out there, waiting. Directly Munro throws the door open, he's shot dead. Given the weapon is the same one, it's the same assailant. Really good odds on that, I'd say. So, why kill Munro, but not you?"

Heretofore I had simply assumed the shooter thought Munro was me. LeMay's train of thought and supporting questions invalidated that assumption. What, then, was left?

I tugged the meat stick from her and took a bite. "He had an unobstructed view of the target," I said slowly, "and a clear shot at it. He knew immediately the door opened that it was not me."

"And yet he fired. Why?" I shook my head, and she went on, "All right, let's move on to you. You arrived in Sayoun five days ago. These events began on the third day. In addition to the shootings, your room was searched. A Scritchy was planted in your door jamb---"

"By Frazier," I broke in.

"You're missing my point, *ma p'tite*. All these actions came . . . " LeMay's voice drifted off, and she gazed down at her feet. Finally she sighed. "You know, I could get used to this. Endearments. I've wondered what it would be like to use them." Her voice dropped a full octave. "To have a reason to use them." She shook her head like a dog emerging from a bath, and gave me a long look. "Sorry. All these actions---"

She stopped when my hand touched her thigh. Under the denim fabric, the long muscle felt as taut as a violin string. I kneaded it gently, my eyes fixed on hers. Like me, she had had relationships, some in the line of duty, some very temporarily personal. Nothing had endured. Not even this present relationship held the promise of lasting any longer than the next three days or so. Time was something we had not discussed-- had yet even to consider--and that omission now stood out in my mind. I began to wonder whether her present thoughts had taken the same tack. Time--in our respective professions there was never quite enough of it. Because it did not exist? Or because we did not, for whatever reason, avail ourselves of it?

Endearments, LeMay had used. Probably she had read them in books or heard them in entertainment 'grams, and she had supposed that two people who had a linkage of affection used endearments in reference to one another as a matter of course, rather like punctuation. But with reference to me, she had uttered them not to end a sentence, but because they represented what she truly felt.

That I understood this rationale startled me even more than the recognition of it. The tangents of my current assignment had driven me far off course. Deven stood at the helm. It was his job to keep my rudder amidships. Even now I could hear his voice in my mind, cautioning me against sentimentality, pointing out the incompatibility of my work with my thoughts of the woman seated beside me, as if she were some thing, some object, that I could not keep.

"Why *can't* I---" I began, and stopped abruptly.

LeMay's pale eyes darkened to the color of mourning doves, and a film of mist made her irises glow. Her voice was a haunted cry for a dove's missing mate. "*Please* tell me what you were thinking just now," she begged.

I pulled my hand away. "No."

LeMay hung her head. Long hair hid her face, but I thought I saw a tear reach the tip of her nose. Suddenly she shot to her feet. "Damn it!" she growled, in a voice half-choked, and strode to the patio door, her spine as rigid as a pike. She did not speak, and if I could have thought of something to say, I would have broken the silence with it. She stood as one entranced, while a couple hundred meters away, phalanxes of waves

116

marched onto the sand to die.

The last thing either of us needed was an emotional display. Toward the evening we might well be involved in a firefight. Certainly we expected to find ourselves in the midst of grave danger. The overall plan, so far as we had discussed it, was simple in conception; the execution of it required a coldness that for the moment seemed to have escaped us. The prospect of a partnership with a woman who found it difficult to separate her feelings from her work set me on edge, and I was uncertain how to resolve it. She might regard my remaining silent on the futon as a rejection of what she felt toward me. If I got up and approached her, an implicit offer of comfort, I risked encouraging her feelings, to the possible detriment of my mission. Between the two options, I saw no compromise.

Gradually LeMay's shoulders slumped. She inclined her head until her forehead rested against the patio door. Her breath fogged the glass. After a moment she drew back just a bit and fogged more of it, and with the tip of her finger traced a heart there, with letters in the center of it.

Satisfied, LeMay gave a little nod, turned around, and returned to the futon. Rather than seat herself, she knelt on the floor and rested her forearms beside me on the cushion, hands clasped together. In this position, she might have prayed. Into the triangle formed by her two forearms and the edge of the futon, she lowered her face.

"I have never been in love," she whispered. "I don't know what it means, or what it is supposed to mean."

"Silver," I said, and waited. After a few seconds she slowly raised her eyes to mine. They were slightly reddened, and wet. For just a moment I regretted what I was going to say, what I had to say. Over my thoughts hovered Deven's stern countenance, reminding me of my identity and my training, and I took a measure of strength from it. "Not now," I told her softly.

Her eyes widened, the glistening pale gray darkening to a dull slate. Seconds passed, perhaps a minute. Her upper incisors sank into her lower lip, without drawing blood, and her upper body rocked gently back and forth while she fought within herself. At last her lips grew taut with resolve, and she drew a huge breath and let it out slowly.

"You're right," she agreed, and I was relieved to note that the quaver was gone from her voice. "I'm sorry."

I badly needed to change the subject. My own feelings were already

117

banging on the boards nailed across the door behind which I had confined them. I was surprised to find them still alive. *Poor things must be starving,* I thought, and swallowed back a chuckle.

The look on LeMay's face said that she had never heard a sound quite like that. I succumbed to a mad moment. "Sausage sticks," I explained, and touched a fist to my heart. Before she could comment, I prompted, "You were going to say something about all these actions."

LeMay pulled herself up onto the futon. Little vertical furrows appeared on the bridge of her nose as she tried to recall the context. Finally she brightened. "All those actions transpired after your arrival and identification," she said. "Grenke might not have known who you were, but he knew what you were. He made an assumption regarding why you had come here. I think he wanted to instill in you a sense of urgency. It did not occur to him that you were here on furlough."

"Urgency," I repeated.

She peered at me. "Remember what Agate told us before she was shot? She said Ecotect would continue to protest, no matter how many of them you killed. And you told me later that Kitch had said the constables wanted to get rid of all of them now. I know the reasoning is convoluted, but try this: Grenke wanted you to act without thinking. He wanted you to take out Ecotect in order to protect Tillvan. He doesn't want you to know that he and his group are the real threat here."

"I think he's failed in that regard, Silver."

"But he doesn't know that!"

I mulled this over. "But what does he gain?"

"You get Ecotect out of the way, you think you've done your job, and he removes Tillvan."

"Which brings us back to those unknown factors you mentioned," I said.

LeMay grinned triumphantly.

"All right," I said. "The shot at me on the beach, okay. Sacrificing Munro in support of that urgency you mentioned, okay. But after meeting me, I think Grenke changed his mind. I was too dangerous. He ordered Frazier to kill me if it could be done with minimal risk. That's why the Scritchy. But I don't think the deaths of those three young men in the bungalow in Makalla were Grenke's doing. Frazier could have killed them, but he denied it, under circumstances that compel me to believe him. So who killed them, and why?"

"Down to one factor, then," said LeMay. "Someone is killing off Ecotect. In fact . . . " She paused for a moment, eyes half-closed. "In fact, with the possible exception of Kitch, Ecotect has been killed off. There were a few hangers-on at the bonfires, but they were there for the free beer. One or two may have been sympathizers, but not dedicated."

"Grenke has Agate killed," I pointed out. "Someone else kills the three men in the bungalow. Noone inadvertently kills himself. That's what we're left with."

"I know, I know." LeMay dragged spread fingers through her hair until all the strands spilled down her back. "And we can't assume our unknown killer has targeted only Ecotect."

"Tillvan is not going to delay his arrival for our convenience or his safety."

LeMay grimaced, and nodded agreement. "How do you want to play it?"

"You go to Emmix and find out if Tillvan has laid on transportation, like we planned," I told her. "You already leased an airfoil from there, so that will give you cover. If he hasn't, you'll provide yours. If he has, you cancel it and tell the clerk that you're his chauffer. Then go on out to the Spaceport and scout around. I'll meet you in the coffee shop."

"And you?"

"It's just past midday. We ought to be in position by about five hours from now. If you spot anyone setting up earlier, commo me." We exchanged codes, and I went on, "Sayoun is an autonomous little satrapy. The Constabulary keeps order here. Right now that's Grenke and his team. There's no overarching authority here on Adenne. The territory to the east is Daramat. It's not really our concern, but I want to ask Deven to have someone come and take care of those bodies in the bungalow. Perhaps they have someone who's willing to take Rigantonio's position."

Even as I said this, Deven gave me a black look in the back of my mind, accusing me of inexcusable sentimentality. To assuage him and to explain my thinking to LeMay, I said, "If a civilian finds those bodies, it could bring some attention to this area. With Tillvan staying here with you, we don't want that. We want a controlled disposition."

LeMay gave me a hard look. "Just tell me you're not going after some of Grenke's people without me."

"How would I identify them, Silver? Aside from Grenke himself, I mean." I stood up, and pulled her to her feet. "I'll leave first, because you have to stay and lock up. I'm going to check out that cove again. Stay in touch. And don't you go off looking for them without me."

"Promise," she said solemnly.

013

Makalla was quiet as I passed east along the glideway. With the pale red sun high and hot, most folks with any sense remained indoors until the relative cool of the late afternoon arrived. One or two people gardened in the shade, and a jogger, an older man who should have known better, was taking exercise, heading toward the coast. Nothing clicked until I reached the old fire station where, presumably, Rigantonio's body remained undisturbed. At that point, the jogger registered in my memory.

Glideway dirt flew as I spun the airfoil around, but by that time he was nowhere to be found. I had last seen him, a florid, round-faced man who looked to be on the verge of a coronary, in the vicinity of the kiosk that had opened early for me. In my line of work, there are no coincidences. I sailed the airfoil past the intersections with the two alley glides, scanning here and there for any sign of movement. He had been attired in a pale blue shirt and gray shorts, and his pale, spindly legs could have reflected sunlight. I stayed alert to those three colors, and in fact a flash of light blue did catch my eye, but it proved to be a towel drying on the back of a patio chair.

I gave it another minute, and concluded that I had lost him. Either the jogger had entered one of the bungalows, or he had recognized me and gotten himself out of sight fast. Even if I took the town apart wall by wall, I was unlikely to find him.

With my glide eastward resumed, I raised Silver and told her whom to watch for. If she encountered the florid man, she was to detain him if possible, or kill him if necessary, and to notify me immediately upon either circumstance. As expected, she did not even blink at the instructions.

After passing the fire station I bore south, along the same route Kitch

120

and I had taken north after our first encounter. Intending for the cove, I might have gone the coastal route, but if it was being watched, I could easily stumble onto an ambush. While the same was true regarding the inland route, at least I had the high ground, looking down into the cove from the escarpment. After setting the autopilot and groundhug apps, I raised Deven. With no need to reconfigure him, I had Niobe the 'skipcomp project him to stand beside me on the bridge.

He was dressed in a tan outsuit that emphasized his nut-brown skin, and although the projection did not include much of his office, I gathered he was standing beside his desk. He did not waste time with preambles. "I gather there has been a development, Lieutenant," he said drily.

First I briefed him regarding the bodies in the bungalow and the fire station, and what I wanted done with them. He agreed, with less alacrity than I had expected. A stern impatience darkened his sharp +features as he waited to learn the main reason for the unscheduled communication.

"Round face, red during exercise," I told him. "About a meter-eighty, maybe a hundred kilos. He looks fit enough, even on stick legs. What little hair he has left is gray and short. I spotted a tuft of black and gray body hair protruding from the collar of his jogging suit. Nose is a round knob, lips a little thick. No scars or tats noted." I informed him of the instructions I had given Silver, and added, "So, do we know anyone involved in this assignment who might fit that description?"

"Edam Windle," answered Deven, without so much as a pause to reflect.

I glowered at him. "You *knew*. Sir."

"As of about ten minutes ago, Lieutenant," he said, his tone not quite a rebuke. "His dossier is being uploaded to your Niobe even as we speak. His name came up as the direct result of a search we initiated based on information you provided." Deven paused, glancing ahead, although the limits of the projection field barely allowed him to see past the cowling forward of the plexishield. "I presume we are en route somewhere?" he asked, the suggestion implicit.

I saw no need to go into great detail. "I'd prefer not to make myself a stationary target by hovering, sir."

"Very well. Edam Windle is the past-Manager of Amphictyony Resources Corporation's E&E. He was allowed to retire, under conditions that AmResCor has so far been loathe to divulge. The Kellogg-Feuer whose serial number you provided was traced to him.

Windle maintains a large private collection of firearms, among which are several rifles capable of firing the cartridge you described, including a pair of Marlin 1895s. He has reported one rifle stolen, but has made no mention of the Kelloggs. We are operating under the theory that he did not expect the connection to be made between the Marlins and the Kelloggs, and that, as you pointed out, the theft of the rifle would be relatively easy to attribute to Ecotect, given their reputation as a low-tech organization."

"So he has armed Grenke and his team."

Deven's expression was bleak. "It would seem so. Bogus constables are more credible in uniform and armed with the same weaponry, and Grenke would not have to shop around for illicit sidearms if they were readily available from one source, which is to say, from Windle."

"What's the connection between Grenke and Windle?" I asked.

"Approximately two years ago, Grenke served as a private contractor providing security for one of the projects under Windle's direction. Thus familiar with Grenke's capabilities, Windle hired him for Adenne."

"Do we know why, sir?"

"We do not. Hypothetically, Windle may be trying to establish a lucrative project that will restore him to good graces with AmResCor. But his exact motives remain unclear." Deven paused, and looked at me sharply. "Regardless, your task is to protect Manager Tillvan."

"Yes, sir. I was about to ask, though: should I amend the instructions I gave Silver LeMay?"

"No. At this point, the removal of Edam Windle falls within the scope of your task. While one might lament the loss of information, gathering it is not our function, Lieutenant, nor have we been tasked for it." He paused, and studied me for several seconds. "Was there anything else, Lieutenant?"

I had reached the low range of hillocks where Agate had been killed. I tucked the airfoil behind a crest, where I had a decent view of the escarpment where it overlooked the cove, and brought the craft to hover. "Do we have anyone who could stand in for Tillvan, sir?" I asked. "Someone who resembles, or can be made to resemble, Tillvan as he appears in his records?" A question darkened Deven's already dark eyes, and I added, "Grenke and his lot will be looking for someone who looks like Tillvan to disembark from the *Excel III*, sir. We might derive some advantage by further confusing the issue of Tillvan's identity. Of course, that could place the look-alike in considerable peril, but that's what you overpay us for."

Deven's voice was a dry as the detritus under the airfoil. "Indeed." He considered the suggestion while I kept an eye on the escarpment. Finally he said, "I will have an operative placed aboard. He will have instructions to take cover if fired upon, and to make his way back into the schooner in the hoped-for confusion. I gather there is no need for him to make contact with you?"

"No, sir. Nor is he to interfere in any way with the evolution of events at the spaceport. I don't want him trying to help, regardless of what he sees. For one thing, Silver or I might shoot him by mistake, seeing a stranger armed and firing. For another, Tillvan is not likely the sort who would return fire; normally he has security minions for that. So if the look-alike opens fire, we might as well hang a great flaming sign on him that says, 'I am not Tillvan.' That would start Grenke's team looking elsewhere, and it's likely we'd be the only 'elsewhere' they'd look."

I felt my brow furrow even as the notion formed in my mind. "You could have him stand by afterwards as back-up, sir," I went on. "I'll need his name and commo code."

Deven passed these on to me. I hoped I was not making a mistake in arranging back-up. As I've indicated, Blacklight operatives are an independent lot, accustomed to being in charge, once placed on assignment. Put another way, we take orders from one man. If Grenke didn't kill the operative, I might have to, just to preserve the command structure for my assignment.

"Time is growing short, Lieutenant," Deven reminded me. Doubtless he had read the reservations in my expression, but he made no remark on them. I already had my primary order: protect Tillvan. All other considerations were secondary. "Report when you are in position at the spaceport," he finished, and vanished from the bridge.

In for a penny, I thought, and held to a zigzag course as I made for the cove. Nothing crackled or popped at me during my approach. With Tillvan about to arrive, I had been wondering whether Grenke might take measures to secure the area, especially if Tillvan arrived with security personnel. Neart the crest of the escarpment I set the craft down and disembarked, with Krupp in hand. I crawled on hands and knees to the edge, and peered down at the cove several times, ducking back quickly each time.

Finally, I was able to conclude that the cove was unsecured for the moment, and stood up, frowning as I tried to add the twos and twos of what I knew and pound them into fours. Nothing quite matched up. Grenke had to know the day and time of Tillvan's arrival, but that information, while not common knowledge, was available to anyone with access to AmResCor and who knew what to look for. Leaving the cove unsecured suggested that Grenke had been informed that Tillvan was traveling without an armed escort, and *that* information was difficult to come by. Windle, using some old contacts, could have managed it. But now I had to wonder what else Windle and Grenke knew. Tillvan's description wasn't generally known, but it wouldn't remain obscure long to someone like Windle.

The most troublesome anomaly was the shot fired in my direction on the beach. To prod me into a sense of urgency in carrying out my putative assignment, the removal of Ecotect, Silver had said. As much made sense. But she had also pointed out that Grenke remained blissfully unaware that I regarded him and his team as the greatest threat to Tillvan. With me presumably basking in the satisfaction of a completed mission, he would see no need to secure the cove, at least not from Ecotect. But what did that now signify regarding my assignment?

I reboarded the airfoil and powered her up, then headed in the general direction of the spaceport. The pale red sun had already begun its descent toward the horizon, and the back of my neck and shoulders felt even warmer than the ambient temperature. I dug out the PHL and raised Silver. She was about ten minutes from Emmix Transport.

"I'm about half an hour from the spaceport," I told her. "Grenke hasn't positioned anyone at the cove. I'm thinking that he'll have everyone at the spaceport."

"As back-up for the sniper, probably," she said. "There's an outdoor deli called *Buckley's Chance*. It's located on top of the kiosks, and overlooks the terminal. I'll meet you there."

"Yeah."

"What's the matter?" Silver asked quickly.

"The more I learn, the less I like this."

"Been there."

"Yeah."

"Nyx? *P'tite?*"

"It's okay," I told her. "But I'll be glad to see you. There are some

124

things I want to run by you."

"That's what you overpay me for," she said, laughing as she broke commo.

I braced myself on the bridge of the airfoil and maxed the fanblades, then made straight for the skyline of the spaceport, hard against the eastern horizon.

014

Silver's directions to *Buckley's Chance* proved accurate. An outdoor cafe located on the roof of the row of kiosks, it sported the usual round tables of white plastic with the red and white sun umbrellas, all set around a central service counter. The cafe seemed to cater to the local workers as well as tourists, but only two of the tables were now occupied, two solitary male patrons in their private thoughts, the midday meal having been finished. Neither of the men appeared to have any interest in me. Although it was much too early for either or both of them to be a part of Grenke's pre-positioned team, I could not discount that possibility altogether. I availed myself of a table near the balustrade that surrounded the rooftop, where I could keep an eye on the two men, and where I had a clear view of the terminal and, incidentally, of the airfoil I had docked at the south end of the open lot between the kiosk row and the terminal. The umbrella afforded scant respite from the sun's heat, but did provide a bit of shade. I reckoned the air temperature at around 310K, although with very little humidity. The tall mug of iced green tea that the server brought me along with a small tray of cheese chunks and stuffed olives had already slaked my thirst, but I was going to need a refill--perhaps several of them--if I remained here for long.

The terminal scarcely justified the name. It was a low square building, perhaps twenty meters on a side, that squatted directly east of the kiosk row. It seemed to exist solely to provide shelter from the weather for the arrivals and departures. The flat roof sloped toward the south and away from the doors, to accommodate the flow of rain water. The window along this side of the terminal was opaque at the downward angle from where I sat, although I had the impression that just inside the door stood a refreshment counter. All in all, the structure seemed an unlikely location from which to fire a rifle without being noticed.

It was now 1405 hours. So stated the little rectangular vidscreen set into the surface of the plastic table. It also listed arrivals and departures, in lettering so small that I had to lean over the screen to read it. The *Baton Vert*, a refrigerated cargo schooner, was due in at 1415. The next arrival, *Excel III*, was scheduled for 1830. I thought about raising Silver, and decided against it. If she were still negotiating at Emmix, she needed no interruption from me.

The sun began to heat my left arm, and I tilted the shade umbrella a little more to the west. By the time the *Excel III* arrived, the sun would be approaching the western horizon. A ground firing position in that direction would be difficult to spot. Near the western edge of the spaceport, about 200 meters away, stood a one-level stay-the-night that a banner draped over the roof flashing proclaimed to be *Knorr's Choice*. The place might also afford some firing security, although any position inside or on top of a building limited the possibilities of escape after the deed was done. Another stay-the-night, at the southern edge and directly behind me and the kiosks, did not allow a proper sighting angle-- the terminal obstructed any view from there. That left only the mobile maintenance derrick.

Just as I turned my attention to the derrick, it began to move into position to service the *Baton Vert* that was about to arrive. Alongside it rolled a cargo jack with a forklift assembly. The operator looked familiar, and a couple seconds later his name came to me: Danelik Thone, the muscle Silver had laid on for odd jobs.

There are no coincidences. Thone's occupation made it perfectly proper and logical for him to be here at this time, operating the cargo jack. Such had been his job for years. Had Silver LeMay cultivated a relationship with him for that very reason? *If there's a problem, Thone handles it*, she had told me. In his capacity as jack operator he could get close enough to Manager Tillvan that a rifle would be superfluous.

Annoyed, I sat back in the chair. Suspicion kills relationships. It also keeps an operative alive. Silver LeMay had been correct in one respect: implicitly, I had come to trust her. Now I had to decide between suspicion and trust. If Silver's loyalty was to me, then Thone was here working, and nothing more; if not, then Thone was at least laying groundwork for Silver's kill. The choices were clear: listen to my training, or listen to my heart.

A blast of air interrupted my decision-making process--the *Baton Vert* had arrived, a forty-meter-long ovoid as green as its namesake, some hundred meters away, emerging abruptly from Track at precise coordinates on the concrete flats beyond the terminal. The blast made the tea in my mug tremble and blew a few strands of hair out of place, and tugged against the umbrella without much effect. Immediately following the blast I also heard just a small impact as the craft settled to the ground. The captain was skilled; he had brought the schooner out of Track no more than a couple centimeters above the surface, and the drop was not enough even to break wafer-thin ceramics, if such was his cargo. More likely, refrigerated, the craft was carrying dairy products and other perishables. The eggs would scarcely notice the jostle.

The maintenance derrick drew up to the schooner's starboard bow, perhaps so that a mech-tech might adjust a sensor array on the hull. Thone, operating the jack with nonchalant skill, approached the port quarter ramp now being extruded from the hull, and prepared to acquire plastic shipping skids. I glanced at the time on the vidscreen: 1416. The captain was also punctual.

The next entry on the screen froze my heart momentarily. The *Excel III*'s arrival had been advanced to 1420. Even as I took in this new information and started to rise from the table, my PHL signaled an incoming message. I hoped it was Silver; instead, Deven announced himself, and I sat back down.

As tempting as it was to reconfigure Deven to a small block of smoked gouda on my cheese plate, I instructed Niobe to permit visual on his end, not on mine. "I have a developing situation, sir," I told him, without explanation.

His voice came softly through the PHL. "I daresay I'm aware of it, Lieutenant. The arrival of the *Excel III* has been moved to a couple of minutes from now. We were advised of this mere seconds ago," he added. His words conveyed more apology than his tone, which was more than I expected. Deven does not apologize; Blacklight operatives are expected to cope.

Already I had gotten back up and was moving swiftly for the staircase that led down to the surface. Neither of the two men gave me as much as a glance. "The look-alike, sir?" I asked Deven. "And did Tillvan alter his appearance?"

"We were unable to place an operative on board," said Deven. "And Manager Tillvan was instructed regarding his appearance, but we did not receive confirmation that he would in fact comply."

I swore, and added, "Sir."

"Understood," Deven said dryly. "Report as soon as you can."

At the bottom of the stairs I raised Silver, my heart having overridden my training without inquiring beforehand as to my decision. She accurately read the tone in my voice. "Where are you?" I asked.

"Five minutes. What's wrong?"

"Tillvan arrives in two minutes, maybe three," I told her. "Check the western perimeter and that stay-the-night for the shooter. There's no look-alike. We're on our own. Keep the mike open," I finished. "Out."

Bright sunlight flooded me as I emerged from the stairwell and onto the concrete surface north of the kiosks. I had no idea of the disposition of Grenke's people, or even if they were in place. With Silver arriving about three minutes too late, I had no choice but to make for my airfoil and try to acquire Tillvan as he disembarked from the *Excel III*. The exposed position brought a chill to the back of my neck. I had to keep moving. Movement might not help against accurate fire from energy weapons, but a long-range rifle would have trouble staying sighted on me. I darted in zig-zag fashion along the solid north wall toward the northeast corner. Another blast of air told me that Tillvan had just arrived. I turned to look as I was running.

A deep brown schooner not much smaller than the *Baton Vert* had downdocked about fifty meters off its starboard quarter. Thone, the forks of his jack loaded with a pair of stacked refrigerated units, appeared not to notice the *Excel III*'s arrival, but as I rounded the corner of the kiosk row, a blue beam sizzled past me and into the east wall of the end kiosk. Heat seared my left elbow, although the beam itself had missed. I ducked back around the corner, Krupp in hand, taking shallow breaths.

The beam had come from the terminal doorway. Evidently Grenke had been advised of Tillvan's new arrival time, updated information he could only have gotten from Edam Windle. Grenke had begun his operation on Adenne with eight constables, which meant he was now down to five. I now knew the whereabouts of one of them, while all of them by now surely knew my location.

Even as that realization occurred, I heard the distant sound of plastic crumpling. I risked a glance around the corner and saw my airfoil listing to port, smoke billowing from the cowling that housed the power module for the fan blades. The position of scorch marks on the cowling suggested that firing had come from the roof of the kiosk row. I had to figure that at least one of the two men on the roof at *Buckley's Chance* had been posted by Grenke to take advantage of the high ground. A waft of air brought the faint, acrid odor of an electrical fire to my nostrils. Another blue beam from the terminal struck the corner of the kiosk row a meter above my head, showering me with tiny, hot fragments of structural plastic. I swore, and returned fire, then ducked back. Raking fingers through my hair removed the fragments there. I brushed the rest from my cammie pullover. Already the hot plastic had burned several holes in it. My tan was going to be interesting.

I now had the location of two, possibly three, of Grenke's team. On the ground a few meters away from me, the shadow of the kiosks darkened the concrete surface. The north balustrade was clearly outlined there, as yet unbroken by human figures. It was only a matter of time before someone leaned over the balustrade to get a better shot at me. Against the north wall of the kiosk row, I was still over-exposed, but with the airfoil disabled I had nowhere to go. At least no one else had fired on me, so far. I tried to calculate the positions of the remaining personnel. One, somewhere, with the rifle, and probably in the company of Grenke, who would want to oversee the operation while remaining relatively safe from weapons fire. The rifle would still be the weapon of choice for Tillvan's execution, assuming that Windle still wanted the blame to fall on Ecotect.

Where else, where else?

The *Knorr's Choice* stay-the-night at the western perimeter of the spaceport was out of range, unless one of Grenke's team had an ergorifle, which seemed unlikely. It was also a possible firing site for the rifle. The only other serviceable location for a firing point was the maintenance derrick. From where I stood, I was unable to see the operating cockpit, but the mech-tech in the cherry-picker seemed to be focused on adjusting one of the *Baton Vert*'s hull sensor arrays. Beyond the derrick, I could see that a hatch had opened in the stern of the *Excel III,* and several figures had emerged from it. One of them was attired in an outsuit, pale blue or pale gray, very untourist-like, and--like all the other non-combatants in the area--he appeared to be oblivious to the fact that people at the spaceport were trying to kill one another. His overall configuration resembled the realtime description I had of Manager Ashler M. Tillvan.

He was not within useful shouting distance. I had no choice but to risk weapons fire by running toward him, to warn him and perhaps get him back on board the schooner. As I steeled myself for the pain of burns, an airfoil, its blades revved to the max, swept across my intended path and made directly for the *Excel III.* I had no idea where it had come from. It was piloted by a slender young woman with a short cap of dark hair, and attired in a halter and shorts, both ultramarine.

McKittrick Day. Kitch. Tillvan's daughter.

I took a step, and another, and a blue beam from above struck the concrete about five meters in front of me, just past the balustrade outline. Another from the terminal passed horizontally in front of me, and I whirled toward its point of origin and fired in one motion, not expecting to hit anything. A scream of pain exceeded my expectations. I hoped he was at least *hors de combat,* if not dying. Suddenly a human figure broke the shadow outline on the concrete in front of me. I flattened myself back against the wall, mentally daring him to lean over the edge of the roof and fire. How brave was he? I dared not divert my attention from him, but my peripheral vision noted that Kitch had already reached her father.

"Silver," I said quietly.

"Three minutes. A bit less." Anguish and frustration lifted the pitch of her voice. "I'm maxed out, *p'tite.*"

Only two minutes had passed since I had spoken with her. It seemed a lot longer.

"There's at least one on the roof at *Buckley's,*" I warned her. "Check that western---"

The massive report of a large-caliber rifle reached my ears. I threw a look in Kitch's direction, but the bullet appeared to have passed without effect. Kitch was dragging her father aboard the airfoil while fighting the controls. He seemed to be caught between resisting and cooperating. While I watched, she struck him on the head with some sort of stick, and finished dragging him aboard.

"*Nyx!*" yelled Silver.

"He missed everything," I said. "Did you spot him?"

"Just the report. Western perimeter, but I don't see---"

A second bullet had been fired. With Silver's PHL still open, I heard

130

her curse. Then came the sound of scraping impact, as if her airfoil had been brought down to slide over the concrete, followed by a series of gradually slowing light clicks, as if she had dropped the PHL and it was now skittering away. I scanned the western perimeter and finally saw a skidding wad of red and gold debris reach the south end of *Knorr's*. But there was no sign of Silver LeMay.

And Kitch had sped away with her father and was headed for points north.

015

I pressed tightly against the north wall and kept watch over the shadows on the concrete, assessing. Useless to curse the unannounced change in arrival time or to lament the operational plan now laid waste. Although Kitch had sped away with Tillvan, and Silver had lost her transportation and communication, my own circumstances had not altered appreciably. I had at least wounded one of Grenke's constables, but whoever was on the roof of the kiosk row could cover any attempt by me to dash to a more favorable position.

Given the constable on the roof was armed with a Kellogg-Feuer, the blue beam had a range to dissipation of about thirty meters. I could cover that distance in five seconds. A fired Kellogg required two seconds to recharge for a second beam. In theory, he could get three shots at me before I was out of range. In actuality, he'd get off one wild burst as I unexpectedly dashed away, and one aimed burst that might or might not strike home. At the moment, fleeing seemed worth the risk. But where would I flee to? And to what end? In any case, flight meant leaving at least two live and armed opponents at my back, an action that was sure to get me sent to remedial tactics classes, should I survive it.

I crept toward the corner of the end kiosk until I could take a quick glance at the terminal entrance, about twenty meters away. The door was open. On the ground lay a uniformed constable, face up, both hands clutching his right side just above the hip, and moaning softly. His shirt was scorched there, and blood oozed between his fingers. His Kellogg had come to rest a couple meters away. The constable's uniform said that the firefight was official business. Whoever was inside the terminal--surely two or three attendants, at minimum--had the good sense to keep out of sight.

The spot between my shoulder blades chilled again. Looking down, I caught a glimpse of moving shadow on the concrete. Evidently the constable on the roof had figured out where I might be, and was shifting to a more advantageous position. I was uncomfortably aware that there had been no more reports from the rifle. Stationary, I was vulnerable to both energy and percussion weapons. Whether I wanted to or not, I *had* to move.

I drew a deep breath and dashed for the terminal door. As expected, a hastily-fired beam from the roof struck the concrete nearby. By the count of two I had reached the constable on the ground. Making a show of it, I fired a burst into his head.

On the roof, as I had hoped, the shooter lost his cool and his aim. "You *bitch*!" he fairly screamed, and thumbed off another errant beam. Amateur to the last, he stood ramrod straight, succumbing to his sense of outrage and waiting for the recharge, and while he was waiting I shot him in the nose, disdaining the shot at center mass, where he might be armored. The energy beam burned through to his brain. His body made a meaty impact with the concrete.

Unlike the other constable, he was dressed in civilian clothes. Well, that figured. In uniform, on the roof, he would be conspicuous at a time when he needed to blend in. I wondered whether the other *Buckley's* patron was also part of Grenke's team. I did not have long to wait. Running footsteps gave me advance warning. He rounded the northeast corner of the end kiosk, weapon in hand, and skidded to an alarmed halt as he spotted me. The failure of their maneuver to bracket me remained in his expression after the beam from the Krupp struck his face.

Three down, I thought. Two remaining, and Grenke.

So far, I had benefited from training, adrenalin, and luck, but to close with Grenke I had to promote transportation. I peered carefully into the terminal. Two attendants in white smocks and one customer in local attire had wide-eyed stares for me, or rather, for the Krupp in my right hand.

"I need an airfoil," I said.

One of the attendants blinked. Whatever he saw in my face compelled him to cooperate. He started to reach into a pocket, and froze

132

immediately when I shifted my aim.

"Very slowly," I told him.

His hand dipped inside the pocket and emerged with a port jack. He laid it on the counter above some display shelves containing assorted snacks, and eased away.

Terse statements seemed to be getting results, so I said, "Where?"

He glanced toward the south, where my own airfoil was still smoking. "B-blue and white. In the parking d-dock."

I scooped up the port jack. "There are three dead constables outside," I said. "If you want to join them, follow me."

Moments later I had powered up the blue and white airfoil, after a fashion. The sounds that came from the power module and the rear fan blades forced me to conclude that the craft's maintenance agreement had expired some years ago. A combination of whirrs and ticks persuaded me to abandon my thought of maxing it out. I had to be content with a mere fifty three kph, assuming that gauge was reading correctly. At least the manual controls worked, and I set a course for *Knorr's*, a little over 200 meters away.

Between the kiosk row and the stay-the-night stood a pair of low warehouses that likely served as cargo holding sites. As I drew abreast of the second one, I received energy fire from it, and banked the airfoil out of effective range. The tableau unfolding there on the concrete flats matched up well with the scene I least wanted to see.

One of Grenke's two remaining constables was standing against the side wall of the warehouse. He continued to fire at me, even though the blue beams dissipated harmlessly ten meters away. I ignored them. In the back of my mind I imagined the other constable, wherever he was, taking aim at me, and my shoulder muscles tightened in anticipation. At the moment, however, I could only give him a passing concern, my attention captured by the hand-to-hand combat between Grenke himself and Silver, near the wreckage of her airfoil. During a brief exchange, Silver was forced to give way before Grenke's superior strength and weight. His massive fists reminded me that he liked to beat people to death.

My training and my heart resumed their intermittent conflict. Without a clear plan, I swung the airfoil around, meaning to intervene somehow. The location of Grenke's other constable suddenly became clear, as a blue beam passed across my bow. He was in *Knorr's*, on the second level, and he had an ergorifle. Grenke had not bothered to draw his own sidearm. The mirthless mad grin on his face said that he was going to enjoy pummeling and smashing Silver. As I came out of the banking maneuver, another beam passed just behind me and struck the port taffrail, burning completely through it. I got off a return shot that struck the wall of the stay-the-night just as it dissipated, and saw the constable dodge back from the window. The ultimate resolutions of the dilemma were clear: if I went to aid Silver, the constable with the ergorifle would get me, sooner or later. If I withdrew, Silver could well die at the hands holding the energy weapons or at the fists of a sadist.

Torn between alternatives, I almost brought the airfoil to hover. A third beam punched a hole in the plexishield in front of me, sending droplets of melted clear plastic like rain onto the cowling. Silver abruptly whirled on me and reminded me that I was supposed to be a pro. "Go get Tillvan!" she yelled.

A split second later she spilled forward onto the concrete, felled by a blow to the side of her head. Sprawled there, she looked up at me. "I've got this!" she shouted, long hair swirling as she rolled aside from Grenke's booted foot. She clambered back to her feet, and looked wobbly, but her voice remained strong. When she saw me still hesitant, she screamed, "*Go do your job, goddamn it!*"

My heart now rose to the fore, filled with the need to aid her. I had to force myself to adhere to my orders and bank the airfoil around to the north.

Deven has scant tolerance for an operative who cannot bear to see the consequences of her or his actions--in this case, abandoning a colleague for the sake of the assignment. If you can do it, you can damn well look at it. But I needed no urging from my inner Deven voice; I *had to* look back. My heart demanded at least this of me.

In the final glance I had of the scene, Silver was ducking under another blow from Grenke, her long hair flying, while the two constables had now brought their weapons to bear on her, although for the moment they were withholding their fire. *I've got this*, she'd assured me, but I saw nothing encouraging about the odds. I could only guess whether she would be able to take any of them with her.

It took a huge effort to finally turn away from her suicide task. One or two raindrops seemed to have spilled from a perfectly clear blue sky, landing on my face, and I swiped them away angrily with the heels of my hands. With a little goosing, the airfoil made it all the way to seventy four kph. Through the inexplicably bleary plexishield I glared at the onrushing terrain, blinking in an attempt to clear my vision while I searched for Kitch's airfoil. But it had already vanished far ahead.

Where, I wondered, *would she have taken him?*

And where the hell had she come from?

Belatedly I recalled the Marlin rifle. It had not been fired for perhaps ten minutes. Now I had to reconsider the identity of the shooter. With the constables dead or otherwise occupied, it came down to Edam Windle. A collector and owner, he would know how to operate it. But where was he now? I had not observed any other airfoils departing the area, but if Windle had docked one behind *Knorr's*, I would not have seen it take off. Still, Kitch had a good head start on him, assuming he was following her at all. My present circumstances compelled me to hope that she was getting away. I tried to recall the terrain north of the spaceport. Some hills and plains and a forest came to mind, but nothing that suggested itself as a possible destination for her.

Of greater concern was Kitch's purpose. As I thought back over the events of the past few days, I realized that everyone around me had had an agenda, while I had only a plan based on assumptions, a plan that had been disrupted by an arbitrarily premature arrival on Tillvan's part. Kitch had known of the change, but how had she known? Silver and I had presumed her abducted by Grenke or dead. It now appeared that, unless she was working in connection with Grenke, she had somehow eluded his attentions at the Makalla fire station and taken a few matters into her own hands.

Upon further reflection, I realized that Kitch need not have known her father's exact arrival time. All she had to do was watch for me at the spaceport. When I arrived, it meant that sooner or later, so would her father. She needed only to wait.

None of this answered the question of why, though.

The plexishield had cleared during my ruminations, but there was still no sign of an airfoil ahead. A glance back informed me that I myself was not as yet being followed. That came as no surprise. Grenke wanted to take his time and savor the crushing of Silver LeMay. Silver, on the other hand, in an effort to gain more time for me, wanted him to proceed slowly and thoroughly. I ached for her. I could feel the barrage of blows from Grenke's massive fists on my head and on my ribs. Thunderheads filled emotions that I had not been issued. More raindrops fell from a sky that remained inexplicably clear, and I wiped them from my face with the hem of my shirt.

Deven, I thought, *you should have issued me tears with my other equipment, or at least authorized your operatives to cry.*

But Deven was going to put me on desk duty for a decade for my lapses into sentimentality on this assignment, given that I survived it, of course. I took a small consolation from the knowledge that the longer you keep alive someone like me--or like Silver LeMay--the more your own chances of surviving the encounter diminish. It was a bleak hope at best, but in the throes of a consuming desperation, even a bleak hope is better than no hope at all.

With that hope flickering, I was able to dry the rain from my face and focus on the more immediate problem of Kitch. Clearly she had been planning this maneuver, or something very like it, for some time now. If she had a hidey-hole, someplace where she might remonstrate with her father unobserved, it would be impossible for me to discover.

Or would it?

Suddenly I knew exactly where she had taken Tillvan. I banked west, and tried to will a few more kph out of the protesting power module.

016

The groundhug app on the airfoil I had commandeered began to malfunction just as I reached the range of foothills that separated the escarpment and the coast from the rest of the continent. Distracted by the mirage of Silver shimmering above the oncoming terrain, I failed to spot a tall shrub in time, and the starboard skirt of the airfoil clipped it and the craft began to yaw.

The procedure for correcting a yaw is much the same as controlling the slide of a wheeled conveyance: bank in the direction of the yaw. Unfortunately, I was piloting an airfoil that had already proven itself relatively unresponsive to instructions. Ahead lay the upward slope of a foothill, strewn with rocks and spindly bushes. I halved power to the fan blades and stepped aside to port, away from the direction of travel. Upon impact with the slope, the airfoil rolled, but I had already jumped off, landing as I had been taught. However, I had practiced on sand and grass surfaces and on relatively smooth pavement, not hardpan strewn with stones and gravel and dead branches. I did manage to gain my feet after the tuck-and-roll, with only a few scrapes and bruises. They remained numb for a few seconds, then all of them began to clamor for attention that I had no time to give.

After scrambling to the crest of the foothill, I discovered that I had crashed within some 400 meters of the escarpment and the cove. If I had guessed correctly, Kitch had taken Tillvan down to the cove. I had to figure that Edam Windle was somewhere in the vicinity. No one was in sight at the moment, but to reach that cove I had to cross open terrain that might be in the field of fire of a high-powered, scoped rifle, operated by someone who could appear almost anywhere, and aim and fire in a matter of two or three seconds.

In the few moments I took to compose myself, I dug out the PHL and tried to raise Silver LeMay. My heart pounded while I waited, counting seconds. She did not respond. Because she could not respond? I shut my mind to that thought. At last I closed the attempt, and looked toward doing my job.

Training reacquired me. It was a welcome companion that obliterated all but the vaguest after-image of Silver. I darted for the escarpment in an irregular pattern, keeping low, pausing and restarting now and then. By the midway point I was drenched in perspiration. Salt water stung my eyes, and I was compelled to dry them frequently with my pullover. By the time I reached the escarpment, still unfired-upon, I was about ready to melt into a puddle. I even considered taking a dip in the ocean, should the cove prove to be unoccupied.

The cove was occupied.

After taking cover behind a protuberance of dark brown rock, I risked a quick look down at the cove, and dodged back. Tillvan, still in his expensive outsuit, was standing on dry sand at the far horn of the curved beach. He looked pained, but otherwise seemed to be unhurt. Kitch, skimpily attired and sunburned, held a sidearm on him from five or six paces away. The arm holding the weapon was straight, locked at the elbow, and rigid. She was shifting her weight from one leg to the other, and back. I thought her hand was trembling a little, but at this distance--about fifty meters on the downward diagonal--I could not be certain. At the curve of the beach, not quite even with me, and perhaps ten meters behind Kitch, stood the jogger, Edam Windle, still in a jogging outfit, holding a Marlin rifle aimed in her general direction. On the sand of the near horn rested two airfoils. All potential targets were well out of effective range of my Krupp Stern. To interrupt the proceedings, whatever they were, I would have to approach closer. And there was no way to do that without being spotted.

If you can't do something without being spotted, and yet you have to do that particular something, then make sure you are spotted while doing it. That's not a hard and fast rule; sometimes it's an engraved invitation to your adversary to open fire. In this instance, Windle was the danger point. Clearly, he was waiting for something to happen; otherwise, at least one of the two others on the beach would be dead. The standoff offered the possibility that Windle might not shoot at me unless he thought he had to.

Accordingly, I yelled, "Up here!" and slowly rose to my feet, waving my hands. "Don't shoot!"

Even as the words left my mouth, they sounded like lines from a bad entertainment hologram. Windle should have fired, of course. He did swing the rifle around toward me. In the periphery of my vision I saw Kitch whirl, and then spin back to her father, who had taken an ill-advised step toward her. I reckoned that if anyone on the beach fired a weapon, it would be her. That was the last thing I wanted.

Without invitation, I began my descent, picking my way over and around the collapsed rock, and always keeping an eye on Windle. A puzzled smirk had begun to form on his round and red face. He was not quite sure what I was up to, but he was confident that it would not succeed. I felt less secure regarding my own plans here when the possibility occurred to me that it might have been he who fired at me on the beach and who might have killed Associate Constable Munro.

Which meant that Windle knew who I was. It was time to plant a seed of doubt. "I'm not here for you," I told him, as I reached the coarse yellow sand just past the rubble at the base of the escarpment. I started to turn toward Kitch and Tillvan, and the rifle followed me.

"Nevertheless," said Windle, "I'll take the Krupp, and the knife."

"Sure," I told him. Deliberately I lifted the hem of my pullover, and withdrew the Krupp, using thumb and forefinger. "And I'll have back the two AV100 notes you took from my room," I said, as I headed for him.

Windle raised the rifle. "That's close enough. Just put it on the sand there, along with the knife."

I shrugged mentally. Closing to within reach of him was my preferred tactic, if I could get away with it. But he had read that field manual, or at least looked at the pictures. After depositing my meager arms cache, I straightened, and stood still, waiting. Off to my right I was aware that Kitch had moved to where she could keep an eye on me while watching her father. I saw now that her weapon was one of the minis in the Saralie line, easy to conceal, and with an effective range of maybe six meters. From where she stood, her best chance of killing either me or Windle with it was to throw it at us.

I spread my hands. "Now what?" I asked Windle.

His proper course of action would have been to order me to back away from my weapons. Instead, the rifle aim shifted to a point between me and Kitch. "I was about to ask you that," he returned.

Windle's actions marked him as an amateur, which did not reduce the danger he presented, because he possessed skills with the weapon. I had no firm plan as yet, but misdirection continued to offer the most possibilities for developing one. "I'm here to finish taking out Ecotect," I said, with a glance at Kitch, hoping she had enough sense to keep her mouth shut.

Tears welled up in Windle's eyes, the last reaction I expected. He socketed the rifle butt into his shoulder, and aimed at Kitch. With his attention diverted, I dug the toe of my boot into the sand, meaning to kick a clot of it at his face at the first solid opportunity.

"Or are you going to do that for me?" I asked.

Windle's tears were flowing now, and his ruddy face contorted with a pain only his spirit could feel. Suddenly I knew I had missed some vital piece of information somewhere. Edam Windle had an economic agenda, so I had been informed, but he also had a personal one. It had something to do with Kitch. But what was it?

From the perspective of my assignment, Windle could shoot Kitch, and welcome. But he had not done so yet. This tableau had been unfolding prior to my arrival. Why hadn't he fired? What was he waiting for?

I cleared my throat for attention. "Wouldn't it be more convenient for you, legally," I said, "for you to let me do my job?"

Windle shook his head, but the rifle did not waver. Still, he did not fire. Finally he said, in a taut, reedy voice, "She ruined my Aggie. She corrupted her."

"You go to hell," snapped Kitch.

In that moment, every statement and every assertion that had been made to me regarding this assignment came into question. Only Deven's order remained in effect: protect Ashler Tillvan. For now, however, despite the weapons trained in his general direction, he appeared to be in little danger.

"Wait," I said, and held up a hand for emphasis. "Just give me a moment. You can wait that long, can't you?"

Windle's voice was choked. "She took from me my posterity. My grandchildren. My Aggie has a chance to be normal again, if . . . "

A leaden silence followed. "*M'sieur* Windle," I said gently. "Agatha is dead."

Windle stood still for a few more seconds, then jerked as if startled, and slowly lowered the aim of the Marlin to the sand in front of him. His eyes, not quite as blue as his daughter's, bored into my brain. "You lie," he said hoarsely, but with just a touch of uncertainty, challenging me to explain.

"I'm sorry, sir. I was there when it happened. Two days ago." I pointed up at the escarpment. "Not far from here, in fact."

Tears resumed their flow down his cheeks. "You?"

"No, sir. She was shot with a weapon similar to yours, by one of Grenke's people."

Windle staggered back a step. "Grenke?" he repeated, his face screwed up with a hundred questions. "Frankl Grenke? He's here?" I nodded, and he went on, "I hired Grenke a couple years ago for security work. He . . . why would he . . . ?" His shoulders slumped, and he almost dropped the rifle. "I don't understand. Why would he kill my Aggie?"

"Why are you here on Adenne, *M'sieur* Windle?"

He looked at me as if I should have known the answer. "To get my Aggie back. To free her from," and he looked at Kitch, but he said, "from them."

"You're not here about the niobium deposit?"

Windle gave me a blank look. "What niobium deposit?"

Kitch yelled, "That one!" and pointed to the escarpment wall. "That one, damn you."

Windle shook his head. He looked lost. I understood that much; I was feeling considerably lost, myself. All my suppositions had now evaporated. *His exact motives remain unclear*, Deven had said. It seemed possible now that Windle's motives had been unclear because he had not been any part at all of the economic scheming of Amphictyony Resources Corporation and its managers. He was here for personal reasons, for family. Before I had arrived on Adenne, I would have regarded such motives lightly, if at all. But now . . . I did not understand him completely, but I understood more of him, because of . . .

Silver . . .

Do your job, she had told me. It was enough to keep me focused.

Threads of events floated before me as if in a soft breeze, looking for a place to land. I reflected upon them for a few moments. Finally, I saw that if I added an extra thread to the weave, I might begin to make sense of the tapestry.

"*M'sieur* Windle, did you kill those three young men in the bungalow in Makalla?"

"I did, yes." Windle lowered his eyes briefly, then looked directly at me again. "Are you going to kill me for that?"

I shook my head. "It's none of my affair, sir. But I would like to know why."

He licked his lips. "Because they . . . they should have offered my Aggie a chance. One of them should have. But they didn't even make an attempt. She should have had a choice."

"Damn you," hissed Kitch. She remained out of range of Windle and me. In the meantime, Tillvan had drawn a step or two closer to her. I didn't think Kitch would kill him deliberately--like Windle, she'd had plenty of time already to do so--but Tillvan might startle her into firing at him.

I decided it would be imprudent to point out to Windle that his Aggie had made her choice. He had a mindset and a focus about these things. He was not about to listen to any argument save his own. But now he had something new to think about. Kitch had turned his daughter to a relationship he did not approve of, but Grenke had by extension killed her, a far more grievous and inalterable offense.

I had to check for veracity, although I could now guess the response.

Windle had gone to the bungalow heatedly, as they say. He had not wanted to talk, thus the broken door. He had burst in and fired and killed without thinking much about it, acting on his pain and anger. I now understood why he had failed so far to fire on Kitch. With time to think about what he was doing, the act would feel like murder to him, something he could not quite bring himself to do. Kill, yes, if sufficiently enraged, but not murder.

"How did you kill them, sir?" I asked.

Windle patted his hip. "I have a Skoda 505. I-I was afraid the rifle would attract attention. I was afraid someone would try to stop me." Abruptly he paused. "Similar to mine, you said?" he asked, hefting the Marlin. "I had one stolen from my collection."

"It's likely that Grenke found out you owned one, during his business relationship with you," I told him. "At some point, perhaps you took him on a tour of your estate?" Windle's expression confirmed my guess. I went on, "But why did you sell him the Kellogg-Feuers?"

Windle frowned. "No, I sold them to . . . I don't recall his name, but it certainly wasn't Frankl Grenke. He said he was setting up a security project, and . . . " He paused, wincing. "Probably one of Grenke's people, right? Grenke would have known I had quantities of some weapons. He would also have known I'd never sell the Marlin." He held up the rifle as if for display. "The pair was a gift from my father, for my wife and me, may she rest in peace." Now his face hardened, and his voice. "He stole a gift from my father and used it to kill my daughter. My Aggie. My only child."

"Sir---"

But he had already turned away from me and was stalking toward the airfoils.

I let him go. No threat to Tillvan, he had nothing to do with my assignment. I doubted he knew Grenke's location, but he was determined to find him. I gathered up my weapons and turned toward Kitch.

"Stay where you are," yelled Kitch, the hand holding the Saralie mini now visible shaking.

I was well out of her range, but another couple steps brought her and Tillvan within mine. I aimed the Krupp at her father, who had resumed creeping toward her. He now froze in place before I could order him to do so.

"You're supposed to protect me," he said severely. "Your job is to protect me."

I ignored him. Kitch was armed, and she was an amateur. She was also in a bad mood, and with Windle now out of the picture, all of her attention was focused on me.

Had I fired at that moment and killed her, Deven would have wrapped up everything and put a great red bow on it. Unfortunate for Kitch, he would tell me, but a satisfactory outcome. I myself did not understand my hesitation. Silver might have, but she was not here. Except in spirit. It might have been her spirit that stayed my hand.

I said, "What's going on here, Kitch?"

Tillvan sputtered. "I *said*---"

"I know my job!" I snarled, and aimed the Krupp at him again. "If you continue to interfere, I'll shoot you myself. Kitch?"

"He can't have my cove," she said. "He can't have Agate Cove."

"That's not for you to decide, Adelaide," said Tillvan, somewhat reasonably.

She whirled on him, screaming. "You're going to let me have this one! Everywhere Agate and I go, you win. You and your machines and your destruction and pollution and death. You bring in your thugs and your bullies and you take what you want. You *always* win. But not this time, Father, not this time!"

She paused briefly, mouth open and chest heaving while she tried to catch her breath after the outburst. The hand holding the weapon steadied now. "There are uncountable worlds," she told him, the pitch of her voice actually dropping an octave. She sounded hoarse, having screamed. "There is more niobium out there than you can possibly use, ever. And you'll find those deposits, to our sorrow. You'll kill life forms you cannot possibly imagine exist, all for some chunks of metal. You'll find them, Father." She stood now with legs shoulder-width apart and braced, her left hand supporting the weapon in her right. "But I'm winning this one, Father," she told him. "I *have to win* this one."

Tillvan licked his lips. He started to speak, but his throat was too dry and constricted. He swallowed, and tried again. "Adelaide. . . "

Slowly Kitch sank to her knees, and began to sob. The Saralie spilled onto the sand. "I have to win this one, Father," she blubbered, head lowered. "You have to let me win this one. Just this once. Please."

"Adelaide," said Tillvan.

"Please, Father," she whispered.

Tillvan approached her. When she looked up at him, he knelt on the sand. For a long time no words passed between them. They gazed at one another as if each were not yet ready to acknowledge the other, their eyes not quite meeting. It was impossible to tell what either was thinking, but the weapon on the sand had been forgotten.

Presently Tillvan's hand came to rest on Kitch's shoulder. Their eyes locked. "Promise me you'll go back to the university."

Kitch made a series of short, quick nods. "Next semester."

"What will you do here in the meantime?" he asked her.

"I'll find something useful, Father."

He hesitated. "And the protests?"

Regret saddened her face. "Probably not. I'm going to care for my cove. I have to care for it. It's . . . I have to, Father."

A long hug punctuated their accommodation. It ended gradually, lingering. Kitch remained on her knees, but Tillvan rose, and after a look and a faint smile for her, he turned to face me.

"I believe your orders are to protect me until my security team arrives," he said. "Is that correct?"

"Yes, sir."

"I presume you can remote your transport to this location." I nodded, and he went on, "My security team is still on Stamblen. As they will not be coming here now, I'd like to be taken to them. Now, please."

"Yes, sir," I said, and dug out the PHL to remote my *Kuremsha* to the cove.

017

What transpired afterwards back at headquarters on Peter's Gate reminded me why we field operatives regarded desk duties as punishment. The ordeal did not begin right away. I spent the first day at my bungalow at the Bachelor Billets east of headquarters, recording my after-action report, which I transmitted to Deven that evening and after which I dozed off with the aid of several fingers of a Highlands single malt. A series of thin beeps roused me early the next morning to a note on the message screen on my wall that Deven wanted to see me face-to-face in his office. Although I doubted he had spent the night pouring over nuggets of vital information in my A-A report, it would not have surprised me to learn that he had done exactly that. At any rate, the note also assigned me a time to arrive that gave me just over an hour to freshen and dress.

At Blacklight we have about as much use for uniforms as we do for traditional displays of discipline. Nevertheless, we recognize that other organizations follow their own notions of these, and so I showed up for the interview in conservative attire--sepia slacks and a tan silk blouse, and brown sandals--having been cued by Deven that a corporate representative would be present.

Like Blacklight itself, our headquarters does not officially exist. By its configuration, the building appears to be a hotel, located between a spaceport and the outskirts of Foxglove, a mercantile and commercial city on the southern continent of Zelezen. The hotel was originally constructed at the behest of Amphictyony Transportation Corporation for AmTour Division. During the construction process it was discovered that most of the funding had disappeared into a corporate hierarch's coffers. A predecessor of mine dealt with the hierarch. AmTransCor covered the loss by transferring the property to AmSec in return for monetary and other considerations, and Blacklight became, for appearances sake, a tour office. However, the travel arrangements made on the premises have nothing to do with tourism.

I arrived at the designated sterile room at the appointed time, knocked three times on the wall by the open doorway, and entered at Deven's command, the door snicking shut behind me.

The room was one of two small conference rooms adjacent to Deven's office. Furniture had been moved or removed since the last time I had been here, and now consisted of a long hardwood table shored up by eight wooden office armchairs with padding at the body contact points. The blue of the padding was two shades darker than the walls and ceiling. Light from the row of square illuminating panels in the ceiling had been upped to about two-thirds. Full turquoise pile carpeting concealed the hard plastic floor. Two overstuffed chairs, remnants from the earlier furnishings that were done in subdued browns, stood guard against the left wall, where Deven's exit back to his office fitted seamlessly.

Although the room was equipped with holographic mood projections, none had been enabled for this encounter. I did detect a faintly aquatic scent that might have been left over from a seascape hologram, but it could also have been my imagination, fresh as it was from the cove. The only blemish on the walls now was a great monitor, on which might be summoned whatever information was required.

At one end of the table sat Deven. Around a corner from him sat a slight, pale man with light, thinning hair. He looked as if he had spent his life counting things. He was wearing a gray outsuit with cream trim. A round patch on the upper left arm, bearing a stylized red eagle rampant on black, identified the man as a representative of Amphictyony Resources Corporation.

Neither man smiled, or greeted me in any way. Deven made a little gesture. "Sit down, Captain," he said.

I did not question the rank given me. Left with a free choice of six, I took the chair around the other corner of the table from Deven, so that I faced the AmResCor rep. Before Deven could make introductions, the man blurted, "*She* is the agent you assigned this task?"

Deven does not abide the term "agent," nor does he suffer well those who use it. "Captain Nyx is the *operative* I assigned to protect Manager Tillvan," he said tersely, with just enough emphasis on the word in question to insist upon its use. "Captain, this is Manager Jac Jardan of the AmResCor policy review board. He has one or two questions for you. Please answer him directly."

"She hardly looks capable of this sort of work," said Jardan, to Deven. "She looks like a seating hostess at a banking convention."

Deven's face did not change. "Captain, are you armed?"

"Yes, sir."

"So if I ordered you to take out your sidearm and shoot *M'sieur* Jardan, you would have no difficulty in doing so?"

"Of course not, sir."

Jardan started to rise. "Now just a minute---!"

"Sit down, Manager," said Deven. His tone did not brook protests. After the AmResCor rep resumed his seat, Deven went on, "*M'sieur* Jardan, I say this to you in all candor: this is the most dangerous seating hostess you will ever have the misfortune to encounter. Now, ask your questions, sir. She has other duties awaiting, and so have I."

For a moment Jardan looked as if he were about to object. Then he settled in his chair, and folded his hands together on the table. "Very well. Why is Edam Windle still alive?"

"I received no orders to kill him, sir," I answered, and stretched the truth a little. "In fact, I received no orders to kill anyone during this assignment. Quite the contrary."

Jardan drummed his fingers a few times on the table top. "According to your report, Windle attempted to shoot Manager Tillvan at the spaceport, and again at that cove."

"That is not in my report, sir," I said. "What I said was---"

"Yes, yes, that you 'believed' Windle was firing at Tillvan's daughter, Adelaide. But you were hardly in a position to make that determination, being unable to see Windle from where you were cowering. Wouldn't you agree that firing a rifle at Manager Tillvan constitutes a threat to him?"

"If that occurred," I said, "then yes, sir, it would. However, Tillvan proved to be the greatest threat to himself, as I stated in my report, by deliberately scheduling his arrival to coincide with that of a cargo schooner, so that he could use the unloading activities as cover. But he failed to notify his protector in a timely fashion. At the time in question, Tillvan was a stationary target, while Kitch . . . Adelaide was not merely a moving target, but one moving *diagonally across* Windle's field of fire. Had he been firing at Tillvan, he would have hit him. His daughter was a far more difficult shot, especially with his having to lead the target while accounting for a range that increased each second."

"Bah!" Jardan turned to Deven. "Excuses. She's offering excuses."

"I credit her analysis," Deven said evenly.

"But---"

"I credit her analysis, sir." Deven leaned forward, his hands flat on the table. "Captain, your response with regard to the scenario at the cove, if you please?"

I shrugged, and said, "At no time on the cove did Windle aim his rifle at Manager Tillvan."

"That means nothing," snapped Jardan. "Tillvan was in danger from Windle at least from the time you arrived until the time Windle departed."

"By that reasoning," I said quietly, "Tillvan was also in mortal danger from his daughter, who *did* aim a weapon at him. Yet you've made no mention of that, sir." I glanced at Deven. It was his privilege to know my thinking before it was presented to outsiders, but I thought he might grant me permission in this instance, especially as his support of me seemed to suggest that his thinking paralleled my own. "May I present an hypothesis, sir?" I asked him.

Deven made a little gesture. "Go ahead, Captain."

I sat back, and stretched my legs. "Edam Windle was an embarrassment to AmResCor," I said, feeling my way. "I don't know what he did--I *don't care* what he did--but it was enough to make the corporation want to rid itself of him if possible. Perhaps they realized they had paid him too much on a buyout settlement, and planned to recoup some of it after his death."

At this, Jardan sat bolt upright in his chair. I ignored the body language. If he tried to interrupt, Deven would stifle him.

"By an unusual set of circumstances," I went on, "Windle was inadvertently embroiled," and here I saw Deven smile faintly in appreciation of the word, "in the periphery of my assignment. Among other factors, he once had a professional relationship with Frankl Grenke, during which he invited Grenke to his estate, perhaps for a conference. Grenke learned a lot about Windle, information he filed away, to be used later, should the occasion arise." I paused. "In fact, that's probably the back door through which he gained access to---"

"Captain," Deven broke in, and shook his head.

"Yes, sir. Windle's tangential involvement placed him on Adenne. But I'm guessing that involvement only became known to you, *M'sieur* Jardan, when we put a trace on the serial number of a weapon. That alerted AmResCor to a developing situation. During my initial briefing I received several files and dossiers. None of them--not one of them-- mentioned Edam Windle. Yet a day after requesting the trace, when I had occasion to ask for an identity check, I was given Windle immediately." I sighed, deliberately. "Which means, *M'sieur* Jardan, that you or someone in AmResCor made certain that we had information-- and potentially negative information, at that--concerning Edam Windle, that would cause us, and specifically the assigned operative, that is to say, myself, to regard him as a danger point."

Now I leaned forward and looked directly at him. "You hoped I would kill Windle for you," I said softly. "How very convenient. An organization without accountability eliminates your black spot, and you go bounding off with your hands clean."

Jardan began to sputter. Deven said, "That will be all for now, Captain."

I got to my feet, nodded to Deven, and departed from the room, carrying with me all my unrelated, unanswered questions.

On the way back to the bungalow I had to shade my eyes from the midmorning light of P-Gate's orange sun, and found myself wishing I had worn a hat. I recalled a camouflage bush hat I'd worn recently, and wondered where it was now. I began glancing over my shoulder now and then as I followed the walk that paralleled the glideway into Foxglove. Each time I hoped against hope to catch a glimpse of her, and each time I was disappointed.

I thought a meal might break me out of my doldrums, so I proceeded on into the city. At a local market I visited one of my off-duty haunts, an outdoor restaurant operated by a wizened old Korean named Sung, and waited while he deep-fried several shrimp and breaded chunks of onions and peppers in his ancient wok. Breaking my custom, I did not watch him, but focused instead on the shoppers around me, hoping once more to find a tall, slender woman with long pale hair in my vicinity. I wondered what kinds of food she preferred. The meal ready, Sung handed it to me in an ornate plastic bowl, added a dipping dish of a sepia sauce hot enough to ignite a star, and watched, nodding and grinning, as beads of sweat burst from my forehead with the very first bite. I think he is a culinary sadist.

After the meal I returned the bungalow still hopeful, and found that what Stevenson said--it is better to travel hopefully, than to arrive--was spot-on. I coded the touchpad on the wall beside the door, but hesitated to open it, fearing I would find the bungalow empty, despite the impregnable security. Still, I searched the interior, heart-heavy. I told myself I would have to get over this. I needed an assignment soon, something convoluted enough to wake me up, though I was anything but drowsy.

The message screen on the wall beeped again, with another note from Deven. It commended me for a satisfactory completion of my assignment. In my inner ear I heard Kitch sobbing over Agate that night we spent together, her tears smearing the ink on that commendation.

Another note asked me to clear up a few minor details on the A-A report. I sat down at the desk in my computer alcove and stared at the microphone for what seemed several hours. I drank two mugs of coffee, smoked four cherry cheroots, and uttered perhaps two brief sentences in in compliance with the request for details. I may have dozed off for a while.

I slept fitfully that night.

The next day I immersed myself in routine. I had cleared out the cooler before going on furlough, and needed to shop for groceries. Once again, while I walked around the markets, I kept an eye out for her, without any expectation of seeing her. I tried to raise her on the PHL, and failed. By this point I would have reveled in a static hiss. The bleak and utter silence I received instead was heart-rending. When I reached the charge counter to have my purchases tallied, the clerk showed some concern regarding my face, and I explained to her that I had rubbed an itch near my eyes after handling the onions. She accepted this with a doubtful expression.

On the way back to the bungalow I made two stops: one to add a bottle of Balmorie to my stock of single malts, the other at the tobacconist's to resupply the cheroots. The tobacco clerk was filling one of the pipe bins with maple blend when I entered the shop. The aroma was yet another reminder of her, and it lingered long after I returned to the bungalow. After putting the purchases away, I sat on the patio and smoked and drank until the stars came out, after which I retired to the sofa, the bed being unbearable at the moment.

I was still on the sofa the following morning when the message screen awoke me. Deven wanted another face-to-face, in his office this time. He gave me half an hour. The time allotted said that he was concerned with my presence, not my appearance.

I showed up, on time, in black denims and a pastel blue sweatshirt. The denims were clean, but the shirt still bore a couple old stains from Sung's dipping sauce that defied all spot removers that didn't actually dissolve the fabric. Deven seemed not to notice. He waved me to the chair that had been placed in front of his desk, and changed the holographic ambience from a seascape to a mixed forest, an unexpected surrender to his intuition with regard to my state of mind.

His desk, as usual, was sparsely cluttered. One of the items was a palmetto, which he picked up, pecked at with a fingertip, and placed before him where he could refer to data on it from time to time, as needed. Finally he said, "A very unusual after-action report, Captain."

"In what way, sir?"

"I was impressed with the massive quantity of detail," he replied. "As I recall, you are loathe to complete such reports, and typically provide as little as you think I will tolerate. I was, however, particularly struck by the utter lack of details regarding . . . let us say, a tangential matter."

I was able to respond readily enough, having anticipated the direction of his interest. "Some events occurred that I deemed were not germane to the assignment, sir," I said.

Deven glanced down at the palmetto. "So I have gathered. Your vocabulary also appears to be growing." He nibbled at his upper lip, something I had seen him do twice more in seven years, and on both of those occasions he had been hesitant about broaching some topic. "I made contact with some officials in Daramat, the territory east of Sayoun," he said at last, and I was certain that this was not the topic he had been avoiding. "They have dispatched three of their inspectors, as they call them, to Sayoun to field the constabulary until replacements can be hired or trained. Another inspector has been dispatched to Makalla, for the same duration. Fortunately, the occasions of serious trouble in those places are rare.

"I also requested, and received, a report of their inspection of the Port of Equatoria Spaceport. Suffice it to say that what they found corroborates your report. There were signs of a firefight. Two derelict airfoils were located, one burned, the other wrecked. I am informed that the wreck was probably caused by a large-caliber bullet that pierced the rear fan blade housing and jammed the rotation. Other data indicate that the . . . operator may have unwittingly passed across the field of fire.

"Four bodies were found, three of them on the concrete between the terminal and the kiosks, which you accounted for, and one partial in an upper room of a stay-the-night called *Knorr's Choice*."

My heart thumped. "Partial?" I interrupted. "Sir?"

"One of the officials dispatched from Daramat was a supervisor of inspectors, with some thirty years of service," said Deven. "He said he knew of but one similar event. What appears to have happened at *Knorr's* was this. The operator of an ergorifle fired a beam directly into the window jamb from a distance of a few centimeters. The jamb of course exploded, with a massive shrapnel effect. The operator was a young male. His DNA is being processed for identity, but it is not a matter of concern for us."

"He was desperate to fire at a moving target," I said.

"That is the assumption." Deven paused, an indication that he was about to shift topics. "Daramat recovered some records in the constabulary, and transmitted the contents to this office. We have also, thanks to Manager Tillvan, acquired certain other information. Most of it, to be sure, is of no use to us. We are not concerned with development projects, ore sample analyses, land ownership, or get-rich schemes. Briefly, what we have put together is this. Through certain liaisons within AmResCor, Frankl Grenke learned of a deposit of columbite on Adenne that could be readily exploited, and planned to have the extraction process developed once he had established ownership and control of the land in question."

"The cove," I said.

"Indeed."

The double meaning of his rejoinder must have occurred to him, because he did something even rarer than nibbling his lip: he smiled. A flash of one, lasting a split second, but a smile nonetheless. Prudently I refrained from adding my own grin.

All too quickly his sharp, nut-brown face sobered. "AmResCor Security will deal with those who provided Grenke with inside information," he went on. "The project itself has been shelved by Manager Tillvan, who has already reported that the extent of the deposit does not warrant the costs of extraction. That, too, is of no concern to us.

"Two other bodies, those of Associate Constables Munro and Logrin, were discovered inside a freezer locker adjacent to the constabulary. Presumably other matters pre-empted their disposal. There is DNA evidence of a third body having been placed in the freezer locker, a female. Pending verification tests, we presume this to have been Windle's daughter. We suspect that he located her, and took her with him for whatever memorial he intends to perform.

"Of interest to us, because you reported being shot at on the beach, is the bullet that was extracted from Munro. Ballistics samples of both of Windle's Marlins are on record, as per ownership requirements; the bullet was fired by the rifle that was reported stolen. Based on that report, and on the Scritchy in your door, we conclude that Grenke was trying to kill you all along, provided it could be done without attribution. Grenke did not want us to seek him out for having killed one of our operatives."

I raised a hand tentatively, to break into his narrative. "And Grenke?"

"Initially Daramat found no sign of him, or of the other constable. However, late last night, which would be mid-afternoon on Adenne, a ladies' sodality, as it is called, from a church in Shiere, a coastal town further south, was holding a cook-out on the beach to raise funds for charity when Grenke's body washed ashore. There has been insufficient time for a full analysis, but Daramat reports that the back of his head was missing, blown away by a high-powered bullet that entered through his left eye, fired at very close range. Other parts of his body were . . . Daramat used the word 'stressed,' which from their description I take to mean that various aquatic denizens had been feasting. Of perhaps more interest is their initial finding that Grenke was shot after he was dead." Deven stopped for a moment, and added quietly, "I have taken the liberty of asking that we be notified when, if, they make a determination as to the actual cause of death."

I nodded.

"Captain," said Deven, and stopped again. "Nyx."

The use of my name reduced the formality of his next words. I simply looked at him, and waited.

"Our orders are usually very clear and simple," he began, and I had the impression he had thought long on his words, but without having finalized what he wanted to say. "We dispatch our operatives with those orders, and we expect them to be carried out. We cannot, from inside this office, determine in advance all of the conditions and circumstances those operatives will encounter during the fulfillment of those orders. We do provide extensive training, to the point that many actions and reactions become instinctive, but in the end, we trust--we *have to* trust-- in the judgment of our operatives. In the field, circumstances are fluid, and we cannot micromanage. At best, after the training period is over, we can give guidance and, on occasion, issue supplemental orders and instructions that we expect will promote the execution of the assigned task."

Deven was not telling me anything new, but I said, "Yes, sir," just the same.

"Personal relationships are also matters of judgment. If we trust you to make the right decisions in the performance of your duties, then we trust you to make the right decisions in your personal lives, with the caveat that the official duties take precedence--they *must* take precedence--over all other concerns. In training you were drilled to accept that there was no place in your life for interpersonal relationships, for . . . meaningful intimacies, and by and large that stricture obtains. Nevertheless, some of us--myself included, as I know you're aware-- maintain personal lives. Given that you understand the risks and the precedence of official duties, Nyx . . . we, that is to say, I, trust your judgment."

"Sir," I said, and could not say more.

"Earlier I referred to details missing from your A-A report," he went on. "I believe I have just presented my response to what you omitted. While we abhor sentimentality, we cannot disregard the state of mind of our operatives. I will not ask you to amend your A-A, or even to expand upon it. If, upon reflection, you wish to add something, I invite you to do so. I will say no more on that subject.

"Apropos of some of the events of your recent assignment, I asked Daramat to verify a couple of points. As of yesterday morning, local time there, the bungalow on the coast south of Makalla remains unoccupied. Also, a spaceskip whose transponder identifies it as the *Zoraya* was located in synchronous orbit above Sayoun. Her comm did not respond to signals, and she is regarded as a derelict." Once more he paused, and added, "I'm sorry."

I found enough voice to say, "Thank you for checking, sir."

"There is one other matter," he went on. "I'm not quite sure what to make of it." He opened a drawer in the right pedestal of his desk and withdraw a white envelope, which he slid across the desk to me. "That arrived earlier this morning, by courier, having passed through several channels, as you might expect."

I lifted the flap, which was unsealed, to expose a pair of AV100 notes. "Windle," I said, and looked across the desk at Deven. "You haven't asked me any follow-up questions regarding him, sir. Although I don't know anything that would be helpful."

"We have not been asked to concern ourselves with his whereabouts or disposition," Deven told me. "For the moment, AmResCor can deal with it, assuming they wish to do so." He made a little gesture of dismissal. "If I learn anything new, Captain, I'll notify you. Incidentally, that is your rank now. Congratulations."

"Sir," I said, and stood, and left.

I took a circuitous route back to my bungalow. Deven's words had afforded me a measure of closure, and in this line of work a measure is more than we usually get. I didn't like it, and to be honest I took the roundabout way back so I could grouse to myself about it, but by the time I reached my door I had resolved to get back into the processes of my life while I awaited the next assignment.

Those processes included a long and hot and steamy shower. Sometimes there is nothing quite like standing under a hot spray, the heat beating down on the back of your neck. I could have stood there forever. After I stepped away and began to soap down, images of Silver LeMay danced before me, in frozen-frames, and I began to feel a warmth that had nothing to do with the water. But I stopped. I stopped, because I could not use her memory in that way. I have no idea where that morality came from. But I finished the shower, taking only the warmth of the water with me.

As I belted the terrycloth bathrobe, Niobe, my percomp, announced an incoming transmission. I rushed from the short hallway to the front room and turned right, toward the computer alcove and the writing desk. I almost dared not ask the point of origin.

"McKittrick Day," said Niobe.

Having craved to hear another name, I was stunned. It took me a moment to realize who it had to be. "Enable hologram," I ordered, and immediately Kitch stood life-size on the floor just outside the alcove, facing me.

She had found some clothing that fit her gangly frame, and she cleaned up very well. Her intensely black hair gleamed with vitality and with blue highlights. In tank top and cutoffs she might have been any young woman on vacation anywhere. Maybe there was just a bit of nebula behind her eyes, or it could have been the quality of the transmission, but her smile said she had found a degree of happiness, a difficult task under the circumstances.

Behind her, distorted glimpses of the cove flittered in and out of focus, and around her a few children looked for shells on the sand or poked curiously at flotsam. "Thank you," Kitch said solemnly.

"For what? What's going on there, Kitch?"

She gestured at the children. "I have a job, as sort of tour guide," she

155

said, gushing. "I'm showing them the world around them. That AV500,000 fundscard you sent me is going to help *so much*. I think I've found something useful that I can do!"

"Kitch, I didn't . . . I never . . . "

She glanced over her shoulder. "Ooo, gotta go. Kids want to swim. *Au revoir*, you two." The hologram vanished, scarcely leaving an after-image.

I muttered, "You two?"

And spun around . . .

She was standing by the sofa, wearing my myrtle green sleep shirt that on her fell to just above her knees. Her left hand clutched my bush hat.

She said, "You should see your face."

She said, "How did I get in here? Oh, *please*! The day I can't bypass security is the day I bronze my water pistol and set it on the mantelpiece."

I found my voice. "You sent her that money."

She said, "Hey, if I can't have fun with my assistant assassin pay, then what's it all for?"

"Silver---"

"I'll answer one more unspoken question. The airfoil crash damaged my PHL beyond repair. I couldn't get into my own house because of the security tripwires! I couldn't remote the *Zoraya*. Not until I had obtained a replacement and recoded it. I know you've been worried---"

"*Worried*!?"

". . . and I'm sorry, *p'tite*."

"But---"

"No! Absolutely not now. We will talk *later*." She flung the bush hat at me, and I caught it. "Take off that robe," she ordered. "And put that on."

www.ingramcontent.com/pod-product-compliance
Lightning Source LLC
Chambersburg PA
CBHW071345170626
46811CB00003B/989